Publisher's Cataloging-in-Publication Data provided
by Five Rainbows Cataloging Services

Names: Howard, Sheena C., author.

Title: Nina's whisper / Sheena C. Howard.

Description: Philadelphia: Sheena C. Howard, 2020.

Identifiers: LCCN 2020902687 (print) | ISBN 978-1-
7344473-0-9 (paperback) | ISBN 978-1-7344473-3-0
(ebook) | ISBN 978-1-7344473-2-3 (audiobook)

Subjects: LCSH: Lesbians--Fiction. | Sexual minorities--
Fiction. | Abused women--Fiction. | Intimate partner
violence--Fiction. | Suspense fiction. | BISAC:
FICTION / LGBT / Lesbian. | FICTION / Thrillers /
Domestic. | FICTION / Women. | GSAFD: Suspense
fiction.

Classification: LCC PS3608.O93 N56 2020 (print) | LCC
PS3608.O93 (ebook) | DDC 813/.6--dc23.

Cover design and illustration by Rebecacovers
Edited by Teja Watson

Made in the USA

To all the children who deserve better.

Nina's Whisper

By: Sheena C. Howard

YEAR 4: 2021

"No one saves us but ourselves. No one can and no one may. We ourselves must walk the path."
-- Gautama Buddha

"I will fight for him," Page said, stumbling behind me in only her robe, slurring her words. I ran down the front steps—baby tightly tucked at my side, two bags on my back—and made a desperate beeline for my Cadillac Escalade. It was ten-thirty p.m. and one-month-old Chasten had slept through the drama. "I will not let you take my baby," Page said. I used my free arm to keep my wife away from me and the baby, putting some distance between us as she grasped for Chasten. I was leaving for good this time. Although Page was impaired by the fog of numerous vodka sodas, she must have felt it too. She knew I was done.

As I strapped Chasten into his car seat, my brain scrambled to figure out how I would make it to the driver's seat without Page getting to him. We lived on a block full of row homes in an urban area, so the noise wasn't necessarily alarming to neighbors. There were a couple of people standing on the corner, about fifty feet away, but apparently, they didn't think that a drunk and angry woman going after another woman—who was clearly frightened and carrying an infant—warranted their help. At least, not at this particular moment. I strapped Chasten into the back, locked his door, then ran to the driver's side, but by the time I reached it Page had already jumped into the back seat with

2

Chasten, through the other side. She was trying to unbuckle him.

"Stop it! You'll hurt him!" There was no way I'd let her take Chasten out of the car, in the condition she was in. I looked around pleadingly, racked my brain about who I could call. I needed someone, anyone, to stop her. Just as I had come to grips with the notion that I might have to physically knock her out—I'm not a fighter but desperate times call for desperate measures—someone yelled, "Officer! Officer, I think she needs help." I looked up and saw a police car pull over at the corner, about fifty feet away. As a person of color, who grew up in an urban area, I don't trust the police, but boy, was I relieved when they showed up.

The officer was approaching us. Looking at the back seat, I could see that the alcohol had prevented Page from successfully unbuckling Chasten, but she was still trying.

"What's the problem here?" He was buff, light-skinned, with a shiny bald head. I exhaled, relieved that someone was there to protect us. Standing next to the officer, I quickly said, "She's drunk, and she's trying to unstrap the baby from his car seat."

"Officer, this doesn't concern you," Page said, now facing us. I looked to see if the officer had a partner with him, fearing that Page would react violently. She always did have a problem with authority. The officer's partner, a thin, white middle-aged man, remained by the police car, watching from a distance. It was surreal, the night sky lit up with a full brownish-red moon overhead. The moon was so bright, you could faintly see the beautiful mountains that surrounded our little town of Sumneytown, Texas. *How could something so awful be happening, when there's so much beauty surrounding us?*

"Ma'am, step out of the car, please." Page ignored him. "Ma'am, I need you to step away from the vehicle. You are intoxicated." He repeated in a stern voice.

"Mind your fucking business, sir." She'd lost it.

I wasn't surprised. It happened so fast. I swear, before the F bomb even left the tip of her tongue, the officer already had her hands behind her back. Page was twisting and turning and shouting. "Let me go! Let me go! You don't have a right to touch me. That's *my* wife and *my* baby."

Relief. I looked back at baby Chasten, still sound asleep. He was so tiny. So innocent. So fragile. He slept peacefully, belly full from breastmilk. I found solace in knowing that he'd never have to experience anything like this again. He was my motivation to leave for good. I jumped into the driver's seat of my SUV as the officer took Page to the police car. I leaned my head back on the headrest, listening to her berate the police officers. I turned to look at my baby one more time. I thought I saw a tiny scratch on his forehead, from Page trying to grab him, but otherwise he was unharmed. I saw the police officer walking toward me. I rolled my car window completely down.

"Is this your baby?" the officer asked me as he handed me the police report.

"Yes, I'm his biological mother," I said.

"Do you have somewhere safe to go tonight?" I looked at the officer, feeling a mix of emotions—terror, shame, guilt, embarrassment. My own thoughts were drowned out by Page screaming violently as she sat in the back seat of the police car. Even though the windows of the police car were rolled up, I could hear her. She was enraged.

"I do, Officer. Thank you" I said, with my hands resting on the steering wheel, shaking uncontrollably. I took one more peek over at Page and then drove off, thinking, *how did I get here?*

YEAR 1: 2018

"How is it possible, you ask, for love to be greater than the person who does the loving? That's because love defies the rules of reason. It is the only exception."
-- Kamand Kojouri

"I'm so proud of you, Nina."

"Thanks, Mom," I said, holding the keys to my very first home. I was happy, but it didn't seem all that exciting. My mom always said nothing excited me, and she was right. I expected good things to happen, because I worked hard for them. My mom had taught me that effort equaled results.

I was twenty-eight years old, and I had just closed on the most expensive house on my new block—the perfect gift to start off the new year. Everything I had planned for my life had gone exactly how it was supposed to. My house was at the intersection of Sixth and Moore Streets, in downtown Sumneytown, Texas. The side wall of my home, which faced Sixth Street, was part of the city's walking mural tour—a huge painting of Toni Morrison, holding a pen. Honestly, I think it was the main reason I decided to buy the house. I fancied myself a budding writer and I felt honored that my new home was host to her legacy. Tourists stood at the corner all the time, taking pictures of the mural and gawking.

At this point in my life, the hardest thing I had endured was medical school. Late-night study sessions and around-the-clock hours at the hospital during my pediatric residency had led to my permanent position as a pediatrician at Dallas Children's Hospital. The hospital was located right outside of Sumneytown, Texas—the town I had grown up in. Once I landed that job, everything on my bucket list had been accomplished—except for one thing. I was single. Hadn't had a successful relationship—like, ever. Yeah, I had dated here and there, but nothing serious. I'd always figured I would be married and settled down by thirty. Now I had to start prioritizing finding that special someone. A friend once told me, it's no fun on top without anyone to share it with. I agreed.

I felt new to Sumneytown. I had grown up in the town—the urban oasis, as I liked to call it—but left at seventeen to go to college. Now, more than ten years later, I didn't know anyone. All of my close high school friends had moved on. The people who were still there were people I wasn't interested in hanging out with. I was used to moving to new places and not knowing anyone. I had lived in New York, Washington, DC, and Oakland—and always found myself, after a year or so, with a pretty active social life and at least one or two good friends, which had always been plenty for me. Any more than that was too much work.

After being in Sumneytown for six months, I was getting restless. I hadn't found my one confidant and my social life wasn't shaping up like it had always done in the past. Time was ticking, and I was lonely—so lonely that it had literally brought me to tears

12

on a few occasions. I wanted to find my person.

My twenty-ninth birthday was coming up and I decided to do a small dinner with a few close friends. Most of my close friends lived in other states. Steph, my best friend from medical school, promised to come, and my cousin Marc would be coming down from New York for the celebration. Marc and I called each other cuz-friends because even if we weren't cousins, we'd still be friends—that's how close we were. A few other friends from work would be joining too.

So, on March 26, 2018, I turned twenty-nine with a bang. A dinner, an ice-cream cake, a few friends, and in bed by midnight—my kind of celebration. I didn't need much. I'd always considered myself

13

easy to please and prided myself on being easygoing. The dinner was at a restaurant called Swift in downtown Dallas—only about a twenty-minute train ride from my house. I liked Sumneytown for its proximity to a major city like Dallas, but also because it was a small, quaint town with a lot of its own unique history. It felt and looked like a city, within a suburb. Several famous artists and movie stars had come out of Sumneytown, so it was pretty well known for a place with a population of only about 70,000.

The hospital I worked at was in downtown Dallas and being just a quick train ride away from work was heaven. I'd always dreamed of being able to commute to work from an awesome house that I loved, in a small, progressive town that was fairly diverse and appreciated art. I was truly grateful for how far I'd come in realizing my dreams by the age of twenty-nine and felt like my life was just beginning.

After dinner that night, I was happy to know that most of my friends had another party to go to; I didn't have to feel bad about cutting out on them early. Steph and Marc came back to my place, but they were the type of friends you didn't have to entertain—like me. Before leaving Swift, I stopped by the bar to say good night to Mel, an acquaintance of mine, who I had gotten to know from the frequent business lunches and events I'd had to attend at the restaurant. I'd had some friendly conversations with Mel and trusted his judgment. I knew he'd look out for me, if

I needed it. At the bar, he handed me a Jack and soda.

"Mel, you know I don't drink this stuff."

"Yeah, but it's from that girl at the end of the bar. She says happy birthday."

"Um, okay. Who is she?"

"Her name is Page."

"Uh, okay." *"Interesting name,"* I whispered under my breath. I took a sip of the Jack and soda, holding my breath and pushed it back to Mel, wrinkling my nose. "Well, tell her thanks," I said sarcastically.

"You tell her. She bought you the drink. Besides, I always see her in here. Seems nice   enough. She always tips me good. Why don't ya go talk to her."

"Guess I have to now." I went over to the end of the bar, while looking at my phone to see when my next train was coming.

"Noticed it was your birthday," the woman said.

"Yeah, thanks. I don't drink much but I appreciate the gesture," I said, looking up. The moment I locked eyes with her, I was struck. She was beautiful, in a subtle way— the type of person that not everyone would be attracted to. She had a gentleness about her. Her smile was a little crooked, but nice. She had a faint scar below her right eye. I must have been staring at her for a while, when her laughter snapped me back into reality.

17

"You okay?"

"Uh, yes, yes," I said, smiling back. My heart fluttered. I was hooked and speechless. When I'm nervous or scared, I tend to run away from the situation. "Have a train to catch, but maybe I'll see ya around. Later, Mel," I shouted as I rushed out to catch my train with my friends. On the train ride home, I went to Mel's Facebook page and looked through his friends to try to find Page. I couldn't stop thinking about her, which was odd for me. Her smile, her skin, her subtlety.

"Found her," I whispered. Her relationship status said "taken." I couldn't believe it. I felt as if fate had brought her to me, just to make me work for it. That night I lay in bed, contemplating messaging her. I decided against it.

When I woke up in the morning, she was the first thing on my mind. I could still picture her face and her beautiful imperfections. I called Mel.

"What'd you say she does again?"

"Who?"

"Page, the girl at the bar last night. Do you *really* know her? When's she coming in again?"

"Slow down, slow down." He giggled.

"She's cool people," Mel assured me. He told me that she came in often. Sometimes alone and sometimes with friends.

"Next time she comes in, tell her I wanna hook up."

After I was sure that Mel had put the bug in her ear, I worked up the courage to send her a Facebook message: "Sooo, you're taken, eh?" I waited for a reply. The message showed that it was read, but she didn't respond. *"Guess she's not interested,"* I whispered. About fifteen minutes later I got a notification. It was her.

"Actually, I just got out of something."

Yes! I knew it was fate. I *knew* it.

"Sooo, you wanna link up sometime soon?" I asked.

"You mean like a date?"

I didn't really *date*. The word date just seemed like a label, that was restrictive, indicating some sort of commitment, but I'd call it whatever I had to in order to see her again. I was lost in my thoughts when another message filled the screen.

"Yeah, sure. Just FYI, don't think we'd work."

She didn't think we would work. *"Who is she to tell me what would or wouldn't work?"* I whispered to myself. I didn't know it then, but she was right. We wouldn't work. At the time, I took this as a challenge. The universe testing me, seeing how badly I really wanted it.

"Well, let's meet up and see." I said. We made our first date. We'd meet up at Swift.

The first "date" was short. Page messaged me the day of to tell me that she had plans to meet some friends, but wanted to pop by Swift to see me before she met up with them. That made me feel special. She wanted to fit me into her schedule. In retrospect, this was a huge red flag, but back then I didn't value myself or my time enough. So, we met on a Friday night, for about 45 minutes. I still remember the way she smelled when we hugged—like vanilla. A very different, but attractive smell. Our time together was so short that night, it left me wanting to know more, like a cliffhanger to an interesting book. I just wanted to turn the page. No pun intended. I wanted to see what was next. I was intrigued. The only other thing I remember about our first date was the sleeve of tattoos that she had on her arm— such a turn-on. She seemed like a badass and I liked that about her. I'd always liked people who expressed themselves in unique ways, who were different. I was different, after all. If I could I'd get a sleeve of tattoos, but I was too career focused and worried that something like that would jeopardize my professional goals. Right from the start, she seemed to balance out who I was. She was the parts of me that I wished I could be. A little freer, a little more edgy, a little wilder.

After our *date* a week had went by. A few text messages, but she didn't ask to see me again. That Friday night I went out to a party, hoping she'd be there. From her Facebook page, I knew she partied pretty frequently, and there were only a handful of lesbian parties going on any given weekend. Eventually I spotted her at a lesbian party called Heaven. The first time we made eye contact, she ignored me. I didn't take offense. She was gonna be mine soon anyway. No need to rush things. I loved the challenge. *Who wouldn't want to date me?* Toward the end of the night, I saw she was about to leave.

"Hey, hey, Page, when are we gonna hang out again? Wanna meet up tomorrow night?" I asked. She seemed like the type of person that liked spontaneity. Maybe it was her artsy, yet hippie style. Or her constantly changing hair color—one day blond, the next day purple, the day after that, black. I'd done some digging on Instagram and Snapchat. I knew I had to show that I too had a little wild side, if I wanted to win her over. My heart actually began to race, as I anticipated her answer. Not that I would take no as an answer.

24

"Sure."

"Cool, lets meet at nine p.m. At Loco Cabana. I'll be at the bar." Even though I wasn't a drinker, I knew she was. Meeting at the bar would disarm her.

The night of our second date I put on my tightest jeans and heels, and pinned my hair up. A date with Page. I still didn't know much about her, besides what I could find on social media. She kept me in the dark and acted largely uninterested in me. Flirty sometimes, other times standoffish. All I knew was that she was attractive, liked to have fun, was older than me, and had just broken up with her girlfriend. I was longing for someone older than me. I'd always had trouble connecting with people my age. In elementary school I'd skipped a grade, because I was significantly above the reading level. I was the youngest person in my graduating high school class, and by freshman year of college I was just turning 17. Older people always seemed wiser, more willing to engage in deep conversations. So, the fact that Page was five years older than me was a turn-on. I was so enthralled in my thoughts; I didn't realize that I was already at the bottom of my mug of hot tea. It was 9:45. I checked my phone to see if she had messaged. She hadn't. As I looked up from my phone, I heard from behind me, "Sorry I'm late, my friend had an emergency. I would have texted but my phone died." As we hugged, she gave me that subtle yet sexy smile I had fallen for the first night we met.

"You look nice," she said. With the compliment, I had already forgiven her lateness. After all, I didn't have anywhere else to go. I appreciated that she was willing to help a friend in a time of need, even though she had plans with me. From the very beginning, I saw the good in Page and ignored the bad. She signaled to the bartender.

"Let me guess, a Jack and coke?" I said.

"Nah, tonight is a Ketel One and lime night."

Keeps me on my toes, I thought.

"Uh, just vodka straight?" I laughed as I tried to hide my judgment. I prided myself on not being judgmental. Just because I wasn't a big drinker, that didn't mean I had to make someone else feel bad about having a drink. I hated when people made me feel bad about drinking club soda at the bar.

"Sometimes ya gotta let loose," Page smirked.

Must not be something she drinks regularly, I thought. The second date went well. Not only did it end with a passionate kiss, but the passionate kiss was back at her place, in her bed. I slept over, on our second date. This was unusual for me. I prided myself on being able to emotionally disconnect from women. I'd spent my twenties too involved in my studies to have any real feelings for anyone. I'd have a different woman over every week—sometimes three in one week. I was a bonified womanizer, and took pride in it. But now, I was nearing thirty and I had my sights set on Page. I'd never do her that way.

Page had a law degree, though she didn't practice in the courtroom. She never passed the bar exam. She used her degree for consulting, mostly worked from home reviewing contracts for major companies in the entertainment industry. She was well connected to the art and film scene in Sumneytown, because she'd negotiated deals on behalf of companies and the "little people," as she called them, making sure the artists got their fair shake when signing contracts for gigs and such. She worked with artists a lot but her consulting with the big companies paid her bills.

Sumneytown was perfect for her. The town was known for filming big budget movies, for a number of reasons, the most important being its lax rules around city permits for filmmakers. I admired her work. It sounded as if it came from a place of genuine care and concern for the little people. She'd always wanted to be an artist, but had no natural talent, as she put it. Her job kept her connected and involved in the industry. I was a writer when I wasn't at the hospital, so I felt we had some overlap there.

The morning after our date, I woke up and turned over. She was staring at me. As my eyes slowly focused, she suddenly said, "Ewww, get out of my bed."

"Huh?" I responded curiously. Had she not remembered that I slept over? She rolled back over, with her back to me. I lay there, confused. What was she talking about? *That's how she feels about me?* I lay there pondering her comment, as she quickly fell back to sleep. I wasn't insulted. I knew she wasn't referring to my looks. I had been with too many women to even entertain the notion that I was unattractive. I'd never had a problem attracting women or men. My ex had marveled at my smooth "cinnamon" skin, heart-shaped face, chiseled chin and long legs. Still, I didn't know how to respond to her comment. It didn't occur to me to leave or even to be terribly offended. Call it too much pride or not enough pride. I don't know. I'll let you decide. A while later she woke up again, got out of the bed, and went to the bathroom, which was on the other side of her apartment. The living room and kitchen separated her bedroom from the bathroom. I stayed in bed, checking out her décor. She had tons and tons of books. I liked to read too. We had that in common. I noticed *Pedagogy of the Oppressed* by Paulo Freire, one of my favorite books. It reminded me of my days in college. I'd majored in biology and minored in sociology and Arabic. I'd had to read *Pedagogy of the Oppressed* for an upper-level sociology course. Not a typical book to have on your bookshelf, unless you had a specific interest in the psychology of power and oppression. Years later, this book would be eerily poignant in my understanding of who I had become. In it, the author, Paulo Freire, talks about oppression as a form of dehumanizing people – the oppressed. Oppressors seek to control you, divide you from your sources of power, manipulate you and distort the stable foundation of who you are. It's a total invasion, one that does not need to use physical means to gain its end. Although it will, if it feels it's losing its grip on you. Ultimately, though, it just needs to convince you that you have no understanding of your own reality.

As my eyes scoured her bedroom, I became more and more determined to learn more about her. Deep in my thoughts, I realized Page hadn't come back yet. I perked up my ears and heard some coughing coming from the bathroom. I wondered if she was okay but didn't want to pry. So, I just waited. When she finally came back into the bedroom, I told her that she had been really mean to me earlier.

"What was that about?"

"I'm sorry, that won't happen again baby." She then ran out of the bedroom. I heard her feet sputtering quickly, then what sounded like some pots and pans being shuffled around. When she returned, she had a tray of scrambled eggs, turkey sausage and a cup of hot green tea. I sat up, surprised.

"It's for you" she said.

I could barely eat my breakfast, as the butterflies rumbled through my stomach. It was soon, but I was falling for her. Quickly.

After breakfast, she insisted that we have a lazy day at her place. She took the tray of food back to the kitchen and hopped back in bed, under the sheets with me. I smiled and rested my head back on the pillow as she spoke softly into my ear, "I love your body. I don't usually like petite women, but your body feels different. It feels good." *Wow, finally someone who doesn't get defensive when I tell them how I feel.* I'd never been the type to talk about my feelings; I'd grown up

34

internalizing a lot of things. It was always easier to just ignore issues and move on. But I'd learned as an adult that not sharing your feelings was disastrous for a relationship. Page showed me that it was safe. That she was safe. That my feelings were safe with her.

By this time in my life, I had already made two promises to myself: 1. I would do everything in my power to make my next relationship work; and 2. I would always be 100 percent honest and share my feelings with my partner. These were two things I had never done before, but I was ready for a serious relationship, and I knew how to make it work. Effort, result. Just like everything else. Simple. Page had fallen back to sleep. I wrapped my arms around her as I held her from behind. My face rested on the back of her neck and I just held her, thinking about what it would be like to wake up holding her every morning. I smiled and dozed back off to the scent of vanilla that permeated her skin.

Page and I had met in March of 2018. I had just turned twenty-nine. She was thirty-four. It was now August, and Page and I were official. A real couple. Not just a summer fling. It seemed fast, but felt right. Everyone told us we were cute together. I thought so too. She'd met my mom, my dad, and my two brothers. She had even met my uncle, who I had never introduced anyone to. She wasn't perfect, but she was special. I loved how passionate the relationship felt—but passion can sometimes be confused with dysfunction. There's a fine line. She'd moved into my house with me, and we will get to the reasons why in a second. That's when I learned that she smoked weed—and a lot of it. I figured it wasn't a big deal, as long as she didn't do it in my house. I wasn't hip on marijuana but I didn't judge people who used it. I just didn't get the appeal. The one time I tried it, it just made me laugh, eat, and fall asleep—I was so sleepy I couldn't even get up to eat. *Why would I wanna feel like that every day?*

You might be wondering why we started living together so quickly. A month after we met, Page lost her job. Apparently, she didn't get along with one of the other consultants on a joint contract she was working on. He had it out for her and managed to get the CEO of the company to fire her while she was on vacation. At least that's what she told me. I had no reason to doubt her account of it. I couldn't understand what type of person would fire an employee on their week off, especially based on something someone else had to say about her. It seemed cowardly to me and I didn't like cowards. Page said she didn't even see it coming. She was two years into a five-year consulting contract. Just like that, she had no income. She also had no money in her savings account. She was very close to her family, but they were poor. Her mother and father lived together in a rundown town right outside of Sanatoga, Louisiana, where she was from — about a six-hour drive from Sumneytown. Her family couldn't help her out financially. If anything, they relied on her to send money home once in a while. Her parents were both sixty-seven years old and had been together for fifty years, married for forty-nine years. For some reason I believed this meant that Page had more insight than I did into what made relationships work. It might have been a comment she made early on, or my own insecurities about relationships, but I had that notion stuck in my head. Kids who were raised by both parents had better relationship intelligence, or so I thought.

One of the first things I learned about Page was that she had no dependable support system. When Page was broke, she was *broke*. If she didn't have a place to live, she really didn't have a place to go. Her parents didn't visit her in Texas much, but I had met them once. Her father seemed to expect his wife to cook and clean. I didn't like the way he talked to Page's mother, but that was none of my business. I knew she had a big family—seven aunts, an uncle, countless nieces, nephews, and cousins, all of whom lived in generally the same geographic area. It was fun to date someone who had a big family, because my family wasn't big. I knew that whoever I chose to settle down with, their family would become my family. My goal was to make sure that her family liked me.

Family was important to me. My mom, brothers, and I were very close. We were all we had. I'd always appreciated our small, tight-knit family, but would feel the sting of jealousy when I went to a friend's cookout as a kid and saw loads of family members. My extended family wasn't that tight. They'd come around once in a while. My parents' divorce had split the family up pretty badly when I was about five years old. Since my dad bailed right after the divorce, my brothers and I had no real contact with my father's entire family. I kept my friend circle the same way as I grew up: small and close. I prided myself on always getting along with the family of the person I was dating. My mom taught me at a young age to respect everyone. Don't judge. And to be myself. I reminded myself of those three things the first time I met Page's family. My mom never steered me wrong. I'm sure it didn't hurt to be a successful doctor, aspiring writer, own my own home, and show up well put together. Her family seemed to love me right away.

By this point in our relationship, however, I could tell that my mom didn't like

Page very much. She wouldn't say it, but I could tell. I just assumed she didn't like the fact that I was spending more time with Page and less time with her. I couldn't hang out with my mom every weekend, like I used to do before I started dating. I did notice that Mother's Day had rolled around and Page didn't even take the time to give my mom a call or send a text to wish her Happy Mother's Day. I found that odd, as I made sure to at least text her mother to say Happy Mother's Day—it just seemed like the decent thing to do. It wasn't a big deal at the time, but I did take a mental note. Anyway, Page ended up moving in with me less than two months after our first date. First, I was just buying her groceries and driving her to job interviews. When I found out she couldn't pay her rent, I couldn't just let her be homeless. I saw us being together in the future and I felt it was my job to help her through a tough time. I wanted to show her that I was serious about her. I wanted to quell all the doubts she had, that I wasn't right for her. After all, I was certain that her unemployment wouldn't last long—her résumé was way too impressive.

Our time as roommates had not been as smooth-sailing as the first few months of dating. When she moved into my place, I was as supportive as I could be. I didn't ask her to pay any rent. I just asked that she make sure she was doing everything she could to find another job. And she was. She had three job interviews lined up. I was careful not to make Page feel as though she owed me anything. I wanted to make sure that she understood that I was there for her because I wanted to be, not because I expected anything in return. I knew how hard it must have been for her to accept help from me. I was her girlfriend, but we'd only known each other for a few months at this point. I wanted her to know that I was committed to making the relationship work. This, in my mind, was a great way to show it.

I was almost thirty and had promised myself I would make this relationship work, no matter what. The only reason I would break up with her was if she cheated on me. This stemmed from the womanizing ways of my father, which ultimately led to some unpleasant childhood memories. When my dad cheated on my mother, he also cheated on me and my siblings. At least that's how I processed it, as I grew into a teenager and began to understand love and relationships. I thought being cheated on was the worst thing a partner could do—but what did I know?

Tap. Tap. Tap. I heard the sound of water droplets as I slept one night. I hopped out of bed, turned on the light on the night table.

"Oh, no. I have a roof leak."

Page woke up. She looked up at the ceiling, then back at me. She gave me these puppy dog eyes, as if to say, *I'm sorry you have to deal with this.* I ran to the basement to grab a bucket, placed it on the floor under the leak, and hopped back in bed. Page kissed the back of my neck and whispered, "It's gonna be alright." Suddenly, I felt at ease. I was happy to have her there. I fell fast asleep.

The next morning, I woke up at 5:30 a.m. I rolled over and Page wasn't there. The bathroom light was on but the door was closed. I lay there for thirty minutes, waiting patiently to use the bathroom. After an hour, I started to get up to see if she was okay, but I didn't want to pry. I knew how annoying it would be for me if I was in the bathroom and someone knocked, rushing me out. I wanted to show Page that I was a chill, easygoing person to live with. So, I waited. And waited. And waited. I was falling in and out of sleep, momentarily waking up to see if she was still in the bathroom. She was. I wondered if she was in there doing drugs. Then I felt bad for having such a negative thought about her. I had never seen her do real drugs, just weed. *What else do people do in the bathroom for this long?*

Eventually, I woke up for good at nine a.m. and Page was in the living room watching TV. I never asked her what she was doing. It just didn't seem important enough at the time. A few days passed and I found a roofer to fix my leak. I needed an entirely new roof. The work would start the very next day. I liked to handle things quickly, especially when it came to the upkeep of my house. I let Page know that the next morning, at six a.m., the roofers would be up there working. It was the beginning of November, and usually temperatures dropped to around sixty degrees at this time of year in Sumneytown. The next morning, the roofers started promptly. They were loud but I was able to sleep through it. Page wasn't in bed, but by this time I was used to waking up at all hours of the night to an empty bed. About thirty minutes after the roofers started shoveling the snow off of the roof, Page came storming into the bedroom.

"What is going on?! Wake up right now!" I popped up out of my sleep, startled.

"What?? What happened?? What's wrong??" Half awake, half asleep.

"Why are they on the roof? What are they doing?"

"I told you I was getting the roof replaced this morning."

Page stormed out of the bedroom, to the living room. I followed behind her.

"What is your problem?"

"What is *my* problem?" she said.

I was confused. I started to question whether I had told her about the roofers. I knew I had, but she was so upset I questioned myself.

"Do you know how it feels to be woken up out of my sleep like that?" I asked.

She turned and looked at me with a blank stare. I looked back at her, confused. I turned back to the bedroom to get ready for the day. I still didn't know why she was so upset. I reasoned that the noise of the work annoyed her. I never brought the incident back up, but this wouldn't be her last outburst.

A few weeks had gone by. Page and I were doing well. Each morning I was fascinated to see what she would put on. One day she'd wear MC Hammer pants with a leather jacket and boots. The next day she would wear a black see-through blouse with baggy jeans and Converse sneakers. I didn't have that sense of creativity with my dress— I was what Page called "basic." I found her style of dress to be quirky, just like her personality. I loved it. She wasn't like everybody else; Page had her own style, her own mind. She helped me dress more edgy. We'd go shopping together and she'd pick out all these cool outfits for me. My style had transformed. I loved it. We'd stay up and talk all night. About everything. I could talk to her for hours about income inequality and then move into talking about anime, all in one conversation. I'd never met anyone that I could do that with. She would be just as knowledgeable on both topics, seamlessly and confidently. She seemed to agree with me on most controversial topics. When we didn't agree, it was never an argument. I'd try to persuade her; she'd try to persuade me. We were both equally talented in supporting our positions. Sex after one of these vigorous but fun debates was always amazing. I'd never had that sort of intellectual stimulation from a partner before.

One night we sat up talking for hours about gender identity. She didn't understand why a trans person had to identify as trans. She simply felt that we should throw out the labels and let people be who they wanted. Essentially, people should be able to dress, look, and act how they wanted without even having to identify as a man or woman. I disagreed. I thought that it was important for people to have their own identifiable category. Trans people were trans. Biologically born men were men. Biologically

51

born women were women. I told her, without labels we can't study and research sociological and biological differences, problems and solutions. I argued, the only reason we know about the scary rates of trans people dying due to hate crimes was because we could identify them as trans. As a doctor, biology mattered to me a lot. I needed to know what genitals my patients were born with, in order to diagnose problems accurately. We never did completely agree but after hours of talking it through, we began to kiss passionately. I felt as if we were the only two people on the planet. I lay on top of her, whispering in her ear, "I love you." She looked into my eyes, in a way no one had ever looked at me before, and said "I love you too." At that very moment, I looked up at the ceiling, while grinding forcefully against her body. I saw a light. It flashed, as if it was a sign from the universe. I looked at her, and it appeared that she saw it too. We both closed our eyes, held each other tight as a tear ran down my eye. I didn't know what had come over me. I was crying, but not sad. In fact, just the opposite: I had found *the one*. A foreign concept to me. I didn't believe in *the one* but I believed that if there was one, she was it. We fell asleep after making love. I woke up around ten a.m., and she was there, lying in bed staring at the wall.

"What's wrong?" I asked.

"Nothing, just thinking."

Often, I would catch her staring off into space. She seemed sad. It triggered in me a primitive instinct to cheer her up. Usually, I'd cook her a nice meal, try to make her laugh, or plan a trip for us. She liked to travel; it made her happy. I'd make the plans; she would just have to show up. Be there with me.

I liked making plans. Ever since I was a little girl and my mom let me plan an entire trip to Disney World, I was hooked on planning. This was my way of taking care of her, which I thought was important because I wasn't the most physically affectionate person and I could be emotionally distant at times. It was just my personality, but I knew my strengths and weaknesses and was very keen on balancing those in a relationship.

"Did you feel that last night? There was a light," I said.

She just stared at me. After about sixty seconds of silence, she said, "Yes, I did. I saw it."

54

I was relieved. We were on the same page. We both had experienced this same divine thing, at the same time. This confirmed that she was worth fighting for. Worth staying with. Worth keeping the promise to myself.

That week, Page had a second interview with a media entertainment company called Insta Tech. She'd be the lead legal researcher and adviser for the legal department if she got the job. I dropped her off at the interview that morning. She looked stunning. I was grateful that I had a job that allowed a pretty flexible schedule. During this time, I was working four days a week, doing ten-hour shifts, which allowed me three days off.

"Good luck, babe! You got this," I yelled as I sat in the car watching her walk into the office building. I felt proud. I knew she'd get it. She didn't look happy. She looked sullen. I didn't understand why someone would be so sad to go to a job interview for a major media company. As far as I was concerned, it was a blessing. I tried to be happy for the both of us. I knew my enthusiasm would wear off on her. The interview lasted about two hours.

"So, how was it? Do you think you got it?"

"I dunno. If I did, I'll have to drive into work every day. They don't offer a work-from-home schedule."

I didn't see any problem with this. I actually thought going into work would be good for her. After all, working from home could be isolating. Having to be up early for work

56

would be a good thing. No more sitting in the bathroom in the middle of the night for hours at a time. She would have to be asleep at a decent hour, in order to get to work on time. On top of that, they were paying a six-figure salary. We'd be way better off with that kind of income coming in. "Said they would call me within a week or so."

"K, wanna go to your favorite restaurant? Made reservations for seven p.m.!"

Her smile said that I knew exactly what she needed. This made me feel good inside. I could only imagine the amount of stress she was feeling. She was in my home and dependent on me for what seemed like everything. I felt it was my responsibility to make sure she was okay. I was happy to take this on; I was secure, had a good job and the financial freedom to help her get on her feet. I had found in Page a partner who was smart, loved to travel, and had a bright future. She was just going through a tough time right now. If I hadn't seen her potential to financially support herself, I would have bailed as soon as she lost her job. In the week that we waited to hear back from Insta Tech, things were rocky.

"Hey babe, my friend up the street invited me to a cookout. Wanna come?" I asked.

"Nah." She was talking on the phone to someone, I don't know who. I really wanted her to go but didn't want to be rude.

"Hey babe, you sure you don't wanna come?"

"I said no, now shut up and go."

I was mortified. *How could she talk to me like that?* I stormed out of the house and went to the cookout. Everyone asked where Page was; I told them that she was home chilling out. I stayed at the cookout for about two hours, the whole time thinking about the way she'd spoken to me. Her tone and words had affected me. On the way home, I got up the courage to tell her how I felt. When I got home, she was upstairs in the bedroom, with a glass of wine. She looked calm and relaxed. I slowly walked into the bedroom, stopping at the doorway.

"Hey babe, I'm back." She didn't even look at me.

"Ya know. I wanted to talk to you about something. I didn't like the way you talked to me when I left earlier."

I was nervous, my voice shaky. Typically, I was an avoider, when it came to these types of things with significant others or friends. I didn't like confrontation, but this was important to me. I knew I should feel comfortable telling my partner how I felt. I knew it was unhelpful to hold things in. I needed to tell her how I felt, no matter what. I had made myself this promise, which I didn't intend to break.

"Look at you, standing there shaking like a little baby," she said as she mimicked a shaking baby, contorting her body left and right. I stood there in the doorway, shocked. I gasped and turned to retreat back downstairs to the living room. I sat on the sofa. I was in disbelief. No one had ever talked to me like that. I'd worked so hard to tell her how I felt in a calm and respectful way. I understood that she might be stressed about the job, about not having any money. But that didn't change how awful I felt about the way she'd responded to me, for a second time. I began to weep. She came out of the bedroom and downstairs, sitting beside me on the sofa.

"Baby, what's wrong? Why are you crying?"

"The way you talked to—" I had tears falling steadily down my face, "—to me." It was uncontrollable. "I just came to you to tell you how I felt, but you humiliated me. You were so mean. I don't understand." She sat and rubbed my back, her eyes looking deep into mine. The house was quiet, making my crying sound much louder and desperate, than it actually was. I was shaking.

"I'm so sorry. That won't happen again. It will never happen again."

I shook my head in affirmation. I was relieved that she had apologized and felt good that she was consoling me. That was the response that I needed.

Over the next year, "that won't happen again" would be something I'd hear often. I learned, from this incident, that she was willing to apologize when she hurt me. She learned, from this incident, that I was weak. Soon after this, she got the call from Insta Tech that she had landed the job. She also got a call from her older brother, Darius.

"Mom's really sick. They don't think she'll make it another week."

Page and I immediately packed our bags to go to Sanatoga. I told the office that I had a family emergency and would be back in a week.

Two weeks after our visit to Sanatoga, Page's mother passed away from liver failure. I wondered why she had liver issues. I remembered that Page had told me her mother was a heavy drinker up until the age of forty-five. I didn't think much of it though. Things don't have meaning, unless they have context. We decided to fly to Sanatoga for the funeral. I requested two more weeks off of work. Four weeks a year was all the personal time I was allotted as a pediatrician. Luckily, Page had two weeks before she started her new job at Insta Tech. We arrived two days before the actual funeral. I was as helpful and supportive as I could be. The day of her mom's funeral, Page was surprisingly strong. I knew she was holding it together for the family. Page was the oldest child of four and the only girl. She was the sibling everyone seemed to rely on. Neither Page nor her family had any money, so I contributed a thousand dollars for funeral expenses. When I told my own mother how I had helped their family, I thought she'd be proud of me, but she wasn't.

"Why don't they have any money? Why did you do that?"

"Mom, they needed help. They couldn't even pay for the food for the reception. I had it, so I helped."

"Okay." She was irked.

I didn't understand her displeasure. I also felt, from this point on, that I couldn't talk to her about my relationship, because even though she wasn't saying it she clearly did not like Page. Unfortunately, this would prove a disastrous calculation on my part.

A couple of days after the funeral, I wanted to get back to Sumneytown. I was tired. I missed my cat, Charlie, who had been home alone for almost a week. I wanted to prepare for work. I was mentally exhausted. I contemplated how to tell Page that I would be heading back earlier than expected. I felt bad, even though I had been there in Sanatoga with her and her family for a few days. At this point, I understood and accepted that Page could be controlling. I viewed it as a character trait that I could live with. There was no other way but to say it.

"I have to get back to Texas."

Page looked up from her computer, staring at the wall in front of her.

"I have to get back to feed the cat and prepare to go back to work. Plus, I'm tired."

"You don't have to be back to work for another week, so don't use that as an excuse." She slammed her computer shut and looked at me.

"I don't really have to give you any reason why I have to leave though." I stood up for myself. "I need to get back. That should be enough," I said.

"Whatever, don't use the cat as an excuse. It's a lame one."

The anxiety I'd felt before telling her had been warranted. Exactly what I thought would happen, happened. She made me feel as though I was doing something wrong. She belittled me. She negated all the support I had given her thus far.

"I found a flight out for tonight." I didn't back down. "I'm gonna get on the eleven p.m."

"Ridiculous." She left the room.

I felt guilty, like I had let her down. *Maybe I should just stay the extra few days and fly back with her*, I thought. I reasoned that she was overly emotional because her mother had just passed. I understood that her and her family's emotions were running high. *It wouldn't be a big deal for me to stay an extra few days, so that we could fly back to Texas together.* She had a point; Charlie would be okay. I could call one of my brothers or my mom to go in and check on her. A few hours later, I told her that I would stay with her. The pattern of dismissing my feelings, and putting her feelings first, would become the standard in our relationship. And a hard pattern for me to break.

After her mother's funeral, Page went back and forth to Sanatoga a couple of times. Work didn't allow me to go, nor did I really want to. Page had been acting more erratic in the days and weeks after her mother's funeral. I could only imagine how hard it was on her. I'd listen when she wanted to talk about it, but I wouldn't ask about her family unless she brought it up. It was a delicate situation.

I developed a habit of being passive, even when I knew I should speak up. It kept the peace. It wasn't like me though. Even though I was an avoider when it came to conflict, I had learned to speak up for myself long before I met Page. My personality, who I was, was altered by this relationship, though I didn't realize it at the time.

YEAR 2: 2019

*"Each relationship nurtures a strength or
weakness within you."*
--Mike Murdock

I remember the day vividly. It was the first week of April, a few weeks before Page's birthday. I was in good spirits. I had planned a five-day cruise for her birthday. Each year I got a fresh new four weeks of personal time off from work. We would spend a day flying to Orlando, Florida, then the next three days on a cruise to the Bahamas, before coming back to Sumneytown. I was sitting in my home office, finalizing the birthday plans, when Page came to the door.

"I found this hair on the bedroom floor."

I looked up and continued to type on the computer.

"Okay." I wasn't sure if she was joking or serious.

"Where'd this hair come from? It isn't yours."

"Um, I don't know. You said it was in the bedroom. Who knows?" I shrugged my shoulders.

She came close to me, with an angry look on her face. I continued to brush her off.

"I'm kinda busy right now, babe."

"Why is a hair that doesn't look like mine or yours in your bedroom, Nina?!" She was serious.

"Who knows." I stood up, now annoyed that she was interrogating me about something so ridiculous. I told her I was going for a walk and needed some air.

"I'll be back."

As I made my way to the front door, she stood in the center of the living room, taunting me.

"There goes the baby, always running away." She continued, "Baby, baby, baby."

I felt myself getting extremely angry. I had learned years before that I could be very mean when I was upset. In a previous relationship, I'd punched a hole in my bedroom wall after my then-girlfriend yelled at me. I can't even recall what she was yelling at me for. I was a hothead back then, but I always felt bad about my violent reaction. I made a promise to

72

myself that I'd never react that way again—no matter what. I actually went to therapy following the incident because I felt so bad about it. I was nineteen when that happened, and had long since learned to use healthy coping mechanisms, like taking a walk and getting some space when I got upset. I've always been hard on myself, and to this day I still feel bad about punching that hole in the wall. It was important to me to walk away before I reached that level of anger ever again. I didn't want to say or do anything that I'd regret. Trying to remain calm, I quietly walked downstairs to the kitchen. I reached into the refrigerator, grabbed a glass from the cabinet, and slowly poured myself some water. As I took a sip, I looked out into the living room. Suddenly, Page's movements seemed to switch into slow-motion. I felt stuck—all I could do was watch. She was staring at me and walking toward the kitchen, enraged. Psychotic, actually. Her eyes were black, as if the whites had disappeared. She walked into the kitchen, standing next to the counter that doubled as a bar. The counter was always messy, with random objects on top of it. She began picking up any object within arm's reach and chucking it at my head. A lightbulb slammed against the refrigerator and shattered right behind my head. A book. A kitchen sponge. I put my arms up, protecting my face. I didn't know what would be coming at my head next. Finally, I noticed a knife in arm's reach of her left hand. Just as I noticed the knife, she grabbed it. She cocked it back behind her head. I retreated further back into the kitchen, now ducking and covering my head, while still keeping my eyes on Page. My back came up against the refrigerator.

"Please don't do it! Please. Please. Please don't do it." I was crying and screaming for my life. Just as the knife was cocked back as far as her arm would allow, she began to throw it toward me, like a baseball coming from a major league pitcher. Just before releasing the knife, she dropped it. There are no words in the English dictionary to describe the feeling of having no control over whether you live or die. Page had taken my life into her hands and I had begged to live. I had begged her for my life, and she had let me have it. I stood up and walked out of the kitchen. I ran upstairs and began grabbing clothes, throwing them in a bag. She trailed behind me. She looked startled, yet emotionless. She was quiet. She just watched me. *Did that really just happen? Did she really just threaten to stab me with a knife?* I ran downstairs with the bag I packed.

"You attacked me with a knife. You need to get out of my house."

She gave no reaction. She didn't acknowledge what had happened. I was shaking. Her expression, however, was as if nothing had happened. I know now that this response was her way of distorting reality. Her reaction made me feel even more disoriented.

"I'm leaving. I'd be stupid to stay in here with someone who just pulled a knife on me.   When I come back you better be gone."

Page ran to the front door and stood in front of it.

"Move. You have to move." I tried to be forceful but calm. I was scared.

"Please don't leave me. I need you in my life. You know I would never hurt you," Page said.

"Please move. Please." I was desperate. After more begging, she finally moved away from the door. I took my bag to my car. I was in disbelief. Breathing heavily. Shaking. I sat in my car and called Steph to tell her what happened.

"That doesn't sound good." Steph was eerily silent, perhaps at a loss for words.

"Yeah, I don't know what I'm gonna do."

I needed someone, at that moment, to tell me what to do. To save me.

"You need to leave her. That's crazy." While talking to Steph, I drove around town. I didn't want to go to my mom's house, because if I told her what had happened, she'd never let me go back to Page. Deep down, I wasn't ready to leave the relationship. I don't know why.

"Steph, I'll call you back."

"Okay, be safe."

As I drove around, I was set in my mind that the end of our relationship had come. I was better than this. I deserved better. I couldn't take it anymore. I began to hyperventilate. The world seemed so small. I looked at my phone and felt I had no one else to call. I

78

didn't want to call my mother, who was my best friend until I met Page. My mother would never say it, but she didn't like Page much, and I didn't want advice from someone who I knew didn't like Page anyway. It wouldn't be useful advice. I couldn't tell my mom the truth of what happened anyway. I didn't want to talk badly about my relationship with anyone. After all, I had told myself that this was my life partner, and if I talked negatively about her to friends or family, they'd judge her and me. That was the last thing I wanted. I needed to protect our image. I also wanted to make my own decisions on my own terms. Close family and friends aren't forgiving when it comes to significant others mistreating their loved ones.

My initial anger and fright began to subside. I couldn't explain it then, and I can't explain it now. I began to reason with myself. I could deal with a little jealousy. In my experience, most women were jealous. I had already known that Page was jealous. I began to feel bad about telling her to leave the house. I always wanted Page to feel like my house was her house too. Exhausted from all of the simultaneous yet contradictory thoughts running rapidly through my head, I began to feel like a hamster, running on a wheel. I reasoned that Page was in an ever-devolving downward spiral. She was always upset. I thought this all related back to the death of her mother. I didn't know what it was like to lose someone close. I figured her instability was just her way of dealing with the loss. I assumed she was depressed. I also told myself that she'd never actually physically hurt me. The mind is an amazing thing. You can talk yourself into and out of anything. Irrational choices seem rational when your reality is distorted.

I decided to drive back to the house. When I walked in, I didn't say anything to her. I was still devastated. I didn't want to talk about it. I just wanted the thought of that knife pointed at my head to disappear. It appeared that Page hadn't thought much about the incident. She was sitting calmly on the sofa with a book in her lap and a glass of wine in her hand.

"When you leave, I feel rejected," Page said.

"You pulled a knife on me!"

She didn't acknowledge this. Emotionless. Oddly enough, when she didn't respond, it made me second-guess my reality. I walked past her and went upstairs to bed. Several days went by. Page never apologized and never spoke of it again. I never brought it back up. I didn't tell anyone, except for Steph. I just wanted to forget it had ever happened. The emotional roller coaster, however, continued. You might be asking yourself; how does someone go on to stay in a relationship like this? At the time, I was asking myself, *how did I even get here?*

"Yeah, you little princess," Page said. "That's what you are, a little princess. Born with a silver spoon in your mouth. Everything has to be your way," she continued.

I can't remember why she was taunting me, but for whatever reason when I came home from work that day, almost as soon as I walked in, she was trying to provoke me. When she didn't get a rise out of me, she'd antagonize me even more. I knew this intellectually, and it infuriated me. I tried to make sense of it all.

When Page and I were dating, we talked a lot about our lives and upbringing. I'd told her that I'd had a great childhood. Yeah, I was raised by a single mother, but I had the best childhood ever. My mom didn't have much, but she was smart. To me, we had it all. My brothers and I didn't know we were poor, because we didn't want for anything. We always had electricity, were raised in a house, and my mom always had a working car and good job. I grew up like a typical middle-class kid, even though my mom raised us on a lower-class budget.

Page knew that a memorable part of my childhood was a banner that my mom printed for me, which said *Nina Is A Beautiful Princess*. It was printed in the late 1980s, when printing a banner literally took twenty-four hours. I was a dark-brown girl at an all-white school, and my mom knew how cruel the world could be to someone who looked different. That banner was the crux of my self-esteem as a child. I knew I was beautiful and I could never forget it. The banner is still on my wall in my childhood room today. So, when Page called me a "princess," I knew she was showing her hatred toward me, and I knew she was doing it on purpose. The thing that bothered me was why. Why would someone who claims to love me purposely want to hurt me? I asked myself this a lot. I never asked her. I ignored her as she taunted me, but I was boiling inside. Of course, there isn't any good reason someone would purposely mistreat someone they claim to love. Suddenly, though, on this day, I turned to her and screamed at the top of my lungs: "You are a fucking nightmare! I hate you and I want you out of my house! Why would I want to be with someone who verbally attacks me? That's what you do. I'm not your punching bag for all of your problems." I ran to the bedroom, packed a small backpack, and went to my office at the hospital. I stayed there for the night, sleeping on my carpeted office floor. I had to work early in the morning anyway.

That night, I tortured myself mentally, trying to figure out how I could have avoided this entire argument. What could I have done different? I knew I shouldn't have yelled at her, called her names, and made her feel like my house wasn't her house, but she was totally out of line.

I had found myself yelling at Page more and more, though. I had begun to hate myself for how angry I could get, but at the same time I knew she was purposely making me angry. To the average person, this reaction is the exact opposite of the reaction I should have been having. However, at this point in the relationship, I took responsibility for everything that went wrong with us, even when Page was completely at fault. I'd always find a way to empathize with her.

Later I'd learn that this is the cycle of emotional abuse that keeps the abused trapped. Not physically, but mentally. It's the wearing and tearing of one's sense of self, one's self-esteem, one's confidence until eventually you no longer trust your reality. At this point, however, I hadn't named my relationship with Page as an abusive one. I just didn't see it back then; I hadn't had enough mental or physical distance from it.

I had a long day ahead of me at work, back-to-back patients. I was so consumed by work, by the end of my ten-hour shift I hadn't even stopped to ponder my personal life. I loved my job and it was a steady sanctuary whenever I had issues at home. When things got really bad on a day off, I'd call into work and tell them I was coming in for the day. I'd even work twelve-hour shifts at times. The hospital would never turn down an extra doctor coming in. Plus, it was extra pay. I got off of work at nine p.m. that night. I decided to meet up with an old high school friend who was in town for the week. I hadn't spent much one on one time with any friends since Page and I got serious. I'd had to fit my social life in when Page was either mad at me or away, because she didn't like me hanging out with friends or family without her. When I was giving her the silent treatment, it was the perfect time to catch up with old friends. I stayed out until about one a.m.—late, for me. When I got back home, Page was there.

"Did you mean what you said? About leaving me?"

By now, I had calmed down and come back to my senses.

"No."

"When you tell me to get out of your house, it affects me," Page said. "I have feelings too. You really have to stop saying things like that. I really think you need anger management classes Nina."

I snapped back, "no, I really don't. You say mean things on purpose, to provoke me. It's like you enjoy it or something. It's really sick." I was standing up for myself. I wasn't letting her get away with the gaslighting—I was speaking up. This felt like empowerment to me. There was a deep place inside, however, that felt like maybe I did need anger management classes. I had punched a hole in a wall ten years earlier because I was mad at my girlfriend. Maybe there was an angry place inside of me. I didn't understand, at the time, the power of the small seeds of doubt and criticism that she could plant in my head, which would grow like wildfire in my psyche. I was always critical of myself—it was what had made me so successful in my professional life. But I didn't know that self-criticism could be turned into a weapon and used by a partner to intentionally hurt me.

"Now why would I enjoy that, Nina?"

Good question. But I didn't say this out loud.

"I'm not used to being treated so badly."

"You don't even know what it takes to have a long-term relationship. I've been in a six-year relationship and my parents were

90

together for fifty years. I tell you things because I know what works and what doesn't. Trust me. You really need to work on how angry you get, Nina."

I plopped on the couch and just looked at her, with my shoulders slumped. I didn't want to talk about it anymore. So, I didn't. I just left it alone.

"Okay. I had a long day at work, I'm gonna head to bed in a few."

"Yeah, I have to get up early too."

With Page working at Insta Tech, she had to go into the office five days a week and she had to drive. She wasn't used to driving, let alone having a car, but it was the only way she could get to work—it was in Downtown Dallas, but on the Southside, which was inaccessible by public transportation. The commute was forty-five minutes, but the traffic made it close to an hour. It sounded to me like a great job, but Page had been complaining about it ever since she started. She didn't like the commute. She didn't like sitting in an office. She didn't like having to drive. I thought she should just be grateful she had a job. I was happy for her, but she wasn't happy for herself.

"Are you sure you can take a week off for vacation? It's so soon after starting your new job." I wanted to make sure that she was set for our upcoming cruise. We were supposed to leave in a couple of days. The last thing I wanted was for her to get fired or something.

"Yes, it's fine. What are they gonna do to me?"

She was so entitled—a trait that was bizarre to me. I often wondered where it had come from. But I didn't probe any further, just tried to look forward to the time together. I tried to remain upbeat and positive about the trip, but it went the same way every other trip went. Argument, after argument, after argument.

May in Sumneytown was always a treat. The backdrop of the Cisco Mountains was extra beautiful in May. The weather stayed steady at seventy-five degrees, practically every day. It was a nice Friday evening. Tourists were outside the house, checking out the Toni Morrison mural when I pulled up from work. I parked on the corner and walked toward the house. Page was sitting in her car, just in front of the house, but didn't see me walk past. I could see her wiping tears from her eyes while she sat in the driver's seat. I walked into the house and waited in the living room, periodically peeking out the window to check on her. I wasn't in the mood to be her emotional support, even though I had accepted that she was an emotional rollercoaster. When she finally walked in the door, she was wiping her eyes.

"Are you okay?"

"I'm just so tired. The traffic was horrible."

"*That's* what you're crying about?" I was perplexed. I thought it was odd that someone who had no job and had been totally broke was crying about having to drive to work, when they were making a six-figure salary. I left it alone, though, and continued reviewing my patient charts for work the next day. *At least she's paying me rent now*, I thought.

I woke up, startled by the sound of someone vomiting. I popped up and looked around anxiously. Page was at the foot of the bed, barfing up green stuff.

"Are you okay?! What's going on?!"

"I'm fine, I'm fine," she assured me, between bouts of vomiting.

"I just took a vitamin this morning without eating and it didn't agree with my stomach."

I was concerned. She often threw up, for different reasons but mostly related to hangovers. She was up all hours of the night but I never saw anything in the house that indicated that she was doing hard drugs. At this point I definitely recognized that she had a drinking *problem.* Sometimes I'd try to tell her this gently. I had even gotten her to take a week or two off from drinking anything at all, but then she'd always binge-drink and get sick the next day. It had gotten so bad that I would rarely go out with her. I'd tell her that I was tired from work or didn't feel up to it, but the real reason was that I didn't want to deal with her obnoxious drunk behavior.

"Do you realize how often you throw up?"

She looked at me with that blank stare. The one where she showed no emotion, yet simultaneously made me feel as though I was the crazy one. It's amazing how impactful no response can be. The notion that she might be an alcoholic didn't occur to me. I'd never seen or been around an alcoholic. If you can't name a thing or a behavior, then it seems it doesn't exist.

"I think we need a safe word. When we are out, I could use the safe word, so you'd know when to stop drinking."

She stared at me. I never knew how she would react to anything I said.

"I'm just saying, when I try to tell you to stop, you just get mad at me. I believe your exact words last weekend were, "You're not my fucking mother.""

"Okay, what's the safe word?" She said.

What about 'strawberry'?"

"Okay, cool."

She's trying. Maybe this will work. At least I had gotten her to agree to it without an argument.

Music blasting, disco lights. I was having a pretty good time. Page was having a great time dancing. I was being vigilant though. Nights out with Page were stressful. I looked over and she was taking her sixth shot of vodka.

"Hey Nina, wanna dance with me?" She slurred her words, grabbing my hand.

Before Page, I used to love to dance and was always down to have a fun night letting loose. I'd come to learn that my version of letting loose was different from Page's.

"Sure, let's dance."

"Woah, let me get another shot first, hold on."

"Hey,   hey,   uh...strawberry. Strawberry."

"What? Huh? What are you talking about?"

I stared at her as she continued to pull me to the bar, away from the dance floor.

"Oh, ha ha, strawberry. Nah, I ain't drunk. Just hang on, I'll be to the dance floor in a minute."

I felt defeated. I wasn't looking forward to what was going to happen after the club. My job was to make sure we got home safe. Usually, when we made it back home, she would cause an argument, then wake up in the morning not remembering anything. I'd wake up hurt and confused. This night was just like the others.

When we returned home, she lit up a joint, knowing that I didn't want weed smoke in my house. We argued, she told me that it was her house too, even though she knew that this was a house rule and had abided by it up to this point, or so I thought. Eventually I just went to bed, while she finished her joint in the living room. Another thing I'd learned to live with. While lying in bed it occurred to me that her long nights in the bathroom were actually her smoking weed and blowing it through the bathroom vent so that I couldn't smell it. I put two and two together. I never asked her about it. The next morning while I was on my way to work, my mom called.

"I stopped coming over to your place."

"Why, Mom?"

"Because Page isn't nice to me and makes me feel uncomfortable."

"So, you just stopped coming over and didn't tell me? How can you complain about not seeing me, when you just decided, without telling me, that you would never come over again?"

"Page makes me feel uncomfortable. She's mean to me."

"Okay, Mom...hey, I gotta go. I'll talk to you later. Love you."

"I love you too."

After work that day, I mentioned the conversation to Page.

"My mom says she doesn't wanna visit me because you make her uncomfortable."

"What have I ever done to your mom?"

"I don't know. That's just what she said." I knew they didn't get along, but I didn't really know or understand why. I assumed my mom just didn't like her for me.

"Well, I'm sure over time it will get better between us. Besides, her house doesn't even have any furniture, it's not like it's comfortable to go over there."

"Well, she doesn't have furniture right now because she's renovating her house. That doesn't mean we can't visit her. I don't even know what one has to do with the other, really."

"When we go over there, there's nowhere to sit. And your mom, all she talks about is work."

I didn't see that what she was doing was ostracizing me from my best friend. I didn't know what the cycle of abuse looked like back then. I was so exhausted. Tired of being in the middle of two grown-ass women. Tired of my mother and what she had told me. Tired of fighting with Page, who seemed to be on my side, except when it comes to our actual relationship issues. Page had no problem getting fired up with me when we were complaining or gossiping about someone else, but as soon as I tried to talk to her about things that mattered to me and our relationship, she suddenly didn't see where I was coming from.

Almost two years into our relationship, I had told myself several times that I was done. That I was leaving. At this point, I had been pleading with Page to stop verbally attacking me. I had been trying to show how she was mistreating me, in order to get her to stop. I still thought she could change and she reminded me often that our relationship would only get better the longer we stayed together. I believed this. I had hope for us. Internally, though, I started to wonder if what I was experiencing was abuse. I didn't think she was abusive because I didn't know what that meant or looked like. Certainly, our communication was a fixable problem. I quickly dismissed the idea of abuse and started Googling articles on how to make a partner listen better. Google is only as good as the items you type in the search bar. I convinced myself that her issue was that she didn't listen—she just wasn't understanding my needs. I'd ask her over and over again to stop talking to me disrespectfully. I had come to the conclusion that she was selfish, and accepted that about her. I didn't need anything from her and I didn't expect anything from her. I just wanted her to treat me right.

One night she told me a story about the final straw that ended her and her ex's relationship. She told me that in a last-ditch effort to save the relationship, she had bought a dog. Page hated dogs, so I found this odd — how would buying a puppy save a relationship? I was impressed, though, that Page would go to such great lengths to save her relationship. I always found the good in her. It allowed me to ignore the terrible situation I was in and focus on her positive side. Plus, at this point I had no friends and family to confide in, who could help me see the abuse. I was too busy protecting the image of our relationship that I wanted to maintain. Now I know that victims of abuse need people to help affirm their reality, but unfortunately, at the time, Page was the only mirror that reflected my reality. She'd told me over and over again during our relationship that she knew how to make relationships work. She indoctrinated me into believing that I didn't know how to make relationships work because my mother and father got divorced when I was a child and because I had never had a long-term relationship before her. I also believed her when she told me that our relationship would get better, the longer we stayed together. This form of insecurity that she brought to the surface was like a scrape on the knee. Like the one you would get when you were a child after falling off of your bike onto the pavement. Each time it tried to heal, you picked it and picked it until the scab fell off and it began to bleed. Eventually, you picked it so much, it became a lifelong scar, that you wore like a badge. Page had come along, opening up this wound after it had healed, after you had dealt with it and moved on. It didn't help that growing up your favorite shows were *Family Matters* and

The Cosby Show. You didn't see families that looked like yours, so what was normal to you, wasn't so, in fact, normal at all. Normal families had a mom and a dad, so when someone comes along and tells you that you are lacking, deficient in some way, you believe them.

Previous to my relationship with Page, I had prided myself on being up-front and honest with my lovers. I had always told women that I wasn't interested in anything serious. I had never led women on, intentionally. However, Page convinced me that it was my inexperience that led to our frequent arguments and my unhappiness—as well as my anger issues. I knew I wasn't happy. I told Page several times that I wasn't happy. I was miserable, but my fundamental belief about life was that any result you wanted could be achieved with effort. Page also reminded me frequently that I was *the one,* and that we were meant to be together by some divine force, outside of our own control. No one had ever told me I was the one. Honestly, I didn't feel like anyone had ever really loved me, besides my mom and brothers. Despite everything, she *did* seem to love me, she just had a funny way of showing it, I told myself.

I had planned a weeklong getaway to Miami for November, because I figured Page would be feeling down. Her mother had died in November the year before. Maybe I felt inadequate in being able to emotionally support her, so I chose to spend money on her instead. By this time, though, she was paying for half of our vacations. So at least I knew she wasn't just using me for my money. I just thought I would show her that I loved her more and better than any of her previous partners. I thought I had enough love to cure every problem we had. I couldn't see that *we* didn't have problems, *she* had the problems.

While on vacation in South Beach, Miami Page randomly said, "Nobody has ever asked to marry me." She had been in an eight-year relationship, followed by a six-year relationship. Nether one of them wanted to spend the rest of their life with her. I didn't find that surprising, but I did think about it often. I felt like what they couldn't handle, I could. I wanted to be the first, oddly enough.

"Well, I've never wanted to get married," I said. "I don't see the reason. If you're with someone, you're with them. What's the point of marriage?"

Page shrugged her shoulders and we began to talk about the fun things we would do the next day. At the end of the vacation, on the way back to the airport, I had to get a rental car. We had taken a taxi to our hotel but we had a couple of stops to make on the way back to the airport so we needed a rental car. I had meticulously planned this vacation. Page didn't have to do anything but enjoy herself. When we got to the rental car spot, there was a line of about three people and the quick kiosk wasn't working. I asked Page to watch our bags while I waited in line to talk to a representative.

"Why didn't you schedule this already?" she asked.

"Huh? It's not going to take long."

Page looked at me in disdain. I rolled my eyes and walked to the counter. When I came back with the rental car receipt, I told her that we had to wait about twenty minutes for the car to pull around.

"I really need you to be more patient when we do these things. You're upset about waiting for a rental car. Really?" I got a rush from standing up for myself. Each time, I thought I was showing her that she wouldn't bully me.

"What are you talking about?" She snapped.

"Your attitude is horrible. I planned this entire trip and you're upset about waiting for a rental car."

"I'm not the one with an attitude. You are. You do this all the time, Nina."

These exchanges over the past two years had often left me confused. My reality was completely distorted. I questioned myself constantly. I was upset with myself constantly. We made it to the airport without talking at all. We'd had several vacations over the last two years and they all ended up the same way. I felt as if I couldn't do anything right. No matter how much I tried, she was never happy. We always argued. It was always my fault. *I could have booked the rental car ahead of time. I knew Page didn't like to wait in lines.* I was used to mentally telling myself that I was the problem, not her. I didn't know then what I know now: people like Page prey on empaths, people who put others before themselves.

When we got to the airport, I told Page that I wanted to end the relationship.

"You're gonna break up with me on vacation? In the *airport*? You have no emotional intelligence. You treat everyone like this. That's why you have no friends."

"I have no friends? What are you talking about? I have great friends."

Page would often tell me that my relationships with my friends were disastrous and that my friends really didn't like me.

"You sound really jealous when you talk about my friends like that. My relationships with my friends and family are

114

great." That was me standing up for myself, or so I thought.

"Yeah, okay," Page replied.

When we landed back in Texas, I told Page that I wanted us to go to couples counseling. I just couldn't break the promise I had made to myself that I would try my best to make this relationship work.

"I don't believe in therapy, but I'll go if that's what you want."

I appreciated that she was going out of her comfort zone to save our relationship. It signaled to me that she would also do anything to make us work.

"You know how much I love you. I'd do anything for you. We are in this together," she said.

That made me feel good. Page would often create this us against the world dynamic, that strangely made me feel good and sucked me further into isolation and a warped sense of reality.

At our first appointment, the therapist had us fill out a questionnaire about how we viewed the relationship. Questions like, on a scale of one to ten, how satisfied are you with your relationship? We filled these out in private. I wondered what Page's questionnaire looked like. I knew it must look completely different than mine. For each question, it was clear that I was completely and totally unhappy. When we finally sat down with the therapist, she asked what our major issues were.

"I have no real problems with Nina."

116

Of course, she doesn't, I thought to myself. *She's the one that is killing me emotionally.*

"My only problem is that she leaves the house when she is mad. I feel rejected when   she does that."

"I think it would be best if you didn't run away, Nina," the therapist quickly said.

MY actions were the problem with our relationship? I leave the house because she verbally assaults me when I stay. Why would I stay in the house when someone is disrespecting me and provoking me? I didn't find anything wrong with removing myself from the volatile situation, but at the time I didn't know how to articulate that to the therapist. I felt the therapist had already made a judgment that my actions were the problem in the relationship. Next it was my turn to talk.

117

"I can't breathe in this relationship. When I get up to go to the mailbox, she asks where I am going. I can't talk on the phone in the house because I'm scared she will get mad at me. I can't go out with my friends without thinking she will start a fight with me. She also has a weed problem."

I was scared of the repercussions I'd experience when we got back home because of what I disclosed, but I needed to be honest with the therapist. I didn't go as far as to tell her about the drinking issues, though—still trying to protect Page. I wanted to tell the therapist that she was either drunk or high all day every day, but I didn't have the guts and I didn't want to make her look too bad. The therapist scribbled some things on her notepad and sat quietly listening during the

hourlong session. I wanted to see what she'd
written. I wondered if her notes validated my
experiences; her words sure didn't. I left that
visit feeling like I never wanted to go back. It
wouldn't help—my reality wasn't confirmed.
Actually, I felt like the therapist was telling
me to accept the way Page was treating me.
Page and I got in the car, and as I put the key
in the ignition she said, "Why would you tell
her that I have a problem? You are so
manipulative."

*Manipulative, that's a good word. That's exactly
what you are,* I thought. I didn't respond. I took
the homework the therapist had given us and
stuffed it in the glove compartment. We were
supposed to work on communicating better.
Page was supposed to make an intentional
effort to tell me how she felt more and I was

supposed to stop leaving the house when we argued. Then we were supposed to write a reflection about the results. I felt the homework was futile and would subject me to more harm than good.

By the time the day rolled around for our next appointment, Page and I looked at each other, both thinking the same thing but for different reasons.

"I don't wanna go back," I said.

"Me either."

We had agreed on something, and it brought us closer together. For a moment, we had something to hate besides each other. I didn't even bother to call and tell the therapist that we weren't coming back. The therapist never called to check on us either, which solidified my feeling that she didn't really care about us anyway.

By this time, my friends that lived in Texas didn't come to visit me unless Page invited them. She communicated with my friends more than I did. Early in the relationship, I didn't see anything wrong with that. I didn't need to talk to or go out with my friends all the time. By the time I'd realized it was a problem, Page had already hijacked my friendships and I had to ask her permission to see friends anyway. They would come over when Page invited them, and I was happy to see them. That was enough for me. This was made easier for Page because when her and I met, I was in the process of making new friends and building closer friendships since I was still fairly new to town. This, combined with my introverted personality made it easy for her to hijack any budding friendships. My closest friends lived far away, so they were largely removed from my daily orbit.

I'd stay up late at night researching articles about getting partners to listen better. I'd send her these articles, but she never acknowledged my emails. Since she dismissed them through her silence, I did too. My world was so small.

YEAR 3: 2020

"This misfortune you find is of your own manufacture. Keep hold of what you have, it will harm no other, for hatred comes home to the hand that chose it."
-- Simon Armitage

By the end of our second year together, I had completely stopped being physically attracted to Page. The smell of her skin disgusted me. It had gone from smelling like warm vanilla, to processed alcohol mixed with burnt vanilla. When she went out, I didn't ask where she was going—I didn't care, I was just happy to get her out of the house. I completely stopped hanging out with her and her friends, unless she begged me. I increased my work hours to sixteen-hour days, with one day off a week. This gave me an excuse when I was home too, because I'd need to be reviewing charts and writing medical journal articles. I was always tired, or at least that's what I told her. I was excelling at work, and had won an award for a research paper I wrote on the effects of soy milk on bone development in babies between the ages of twelve to eighteen months. The paper was recognized by the National Pediatric Association as a top paper in the field for the year 2020. By now, you might be wondering why I stayed with her.

Page would brag to her friends about my achievements, about how good I looked, about how I cooked the best meals for her. This confused me. *How could someone treat me so bad behind closed doors, but be so appreciative toward me publicly?* It felt good to be publicly smothered with love and affection by her. She had to love me, if she boasted about me so often to people, I told myself. I held on to the small things, and they neutralized most of the negative feelings I had toward our relationship. The truth is, I just didn't love myself enough then.

By this time, my mother had completely stopped talking to Page and stayed true to her promise to never visit. I didn't bother asking Page to come with me to my mom's house. I'd see my mom monthly, going over by myself for an hour or two here and there. I never talked to my mom on the phone when Page was around. It was strange though—my dad, who I wasn't close to and rarely spoke to, had a great relationship with Page. I appreciated this, as it did allow me to get closer to him. I didn't know it then, but this dynamic that Page created was intentional.

I was thirty years old, turning thirty-one in March. I was in a long-term relationship. My job was flourishing and I owned my own home. On paper, I had everything I'd wanted to have by the age of thirty. I was happy, except in my own home. I was convinced that relationships last when people compromise. In romantic movies, you have to go through something tragic in order to come out on the other end, happily ever after. That's where I was at with it. If I stayed in a relationship with Page, we would have some good years and some bad years. In a forty-year relationship, you might have fifteen bad years and twenty-five good years. In retrospect, I was so deluded, that this logic made sense to me. The mind is a powerful thing. You can talk yourself in and out of anything. Whether I was making rational or irrational decisions—I was strong-willed. It's a personality trait that has worked well for me, except when it came to this relationship. Being stubborn resulted in me having blinders on.

"I think we should have a baby," Page said.

I looked at her, startled.

"A baby?"

"Yeah, I think a baby would be good for us."

"If we had a baby, you would have to carry it." I wasn't interested in having a baby. Childbirth was my biggest fear, next to a

127

significant other cheating on me. The topic ended as quickly as it was brought up. A few days later though, I asked Page if she seriously wanted a baby.

"Yeah, we have good incomes and more people like us need kids."

"What's people like us?"

"People who have good perspectives on the world and care about other people."

I did think Page treated people particularly well. In fact, when she had no job and no money, she made it a point to still give money to homeless people on the street. She'd even chastise me for not doing so. I should have known then that a broke person, living under my roof, with no money yet shaming me for not giving money to the homeless, was

128

problematic at best. It was annoying but it did give me a glimpse into her heart. I viewed it as altruistic, a trait that was attractive to me. I thought she had a good heart and I held on to that.

Over the years, I'd also witnessed her helping out distant friends in need when she could. It taught me to think more about others too. It was because of her that I started volunteering at the local homeless shelter. Interestingly enough, this was something she was happy for me to do without her.

Even though she hadn't brought the baby subject up again, it stayed on my mind. She had planted a seed. She was good at that. *If she wants a baby and it's that important to her, I can probably use that to help her get off of alcohol and drugs*, I reasoned. This made sense to me.

If she got clean, she would probably treat me better.

I decided that I'd have a serious talk with her about what she would need to do, in order for me to agree to have a baby with her. I'd also suggest that I would carry the baby. Here's how my reasoning went. First of all, biology mattered to me. If she carried the baby, then the baby wouldn't be biologically related to me and I didn't know how attached I'd be to a child that wasn't my blood. Second, I was pretty awesome. How could I not leave an extension of me on earth when I died? I was the ripe age of thirty and I figured if I didn't have a baby now, then I wouldn't have a baby ever. The timing seemed perfect and I was sure a baby would fix our relationship, and light a fire under her to shape up.

"If we had a baby, you would have to stop drinking. No drugs in the house either. I wouldn't want to raise a baby around weed."

"Okay. I can do that. I think a baby that looked like you would be awesome. It would be so cute."

She appealed to my conceit and arrogance, solidifying what I already believed to be true anyway.

"You'd also have to treat me better. I'm not bringing a baby into the world with the way you treat me and talk to me."

"Deal. You know our relationship will only get better with time." She smiled.

Her agreement signaled to me an acknowledgment about how horrible she treated me. It also gave me genuine hope, that a baby would make things better between us. In reality, her agreement meant none of those things. I didn't need any more convincing. I had convinced myself that the world needed a baby me running around and that this baby would fix our relationship. Hope is a powerful illusion. It can distort your reality and motivate you to achieve the impossible. You also have to remember that I had no real context for what a healthy adult relationship looked like. My mom was too busy raising us, when we were growing up. She didn't have time for romance or a significant other. I had no real reference point.

The only thing we needed now was a sperm donor. Luckily, Sumneytown had one of the best fertility clinics in the country, very popular in the lesbian community. They were happy to help same-sex couples have children. At our first appointment at the clinic, the doctor—a short-haired older woman, who walked with a slight limp—did an assessment of my health. They gave me a clean bill of health, which made me feel good. I had prided myself on never doing drugs, with the exception of trying marijuana once when I was celebrating finishing medical school. I also didn't drink, at all. When I met Page, I'd have a drink in social situations, but over the last year I had completely cut drinking out. I knew my body was in tip-top shape to carry a baby. The fact that I didn't have high blood pressure or any other health issue signaled to me that my relationship wasn't having any negative physical effects on me. I used everything in my environment to hold onto the false notion that my relationship wasn't that bad.

"You are the best host for a baby." Page said.

I smiled back and thought about how much I liked it when she complimented me. She'd noticed how well I took care of my body, and I assumed by extension that she'd also noticed how poorly she took care of her own body. A big leap, but I had trained myself to make such big assumptions, in order to maintain this relationship and see the good in her. Ever since we'd embarked on having a baby, we hadn't argued as much.

At the clinic, we found the perfect donor. A bi-racial guy who was five-foot-nine, 160 pounds, with brown eyes. His description said that he had light brown skin, which stuck out to me. The baby would be mixed-ethnicity, which worked for us. We wanted the baby to reflect our diversity as a mixed-race couple. Page was white. The donor had a math degree and his profile said that he liked to fish. His medical history was pretty clean, with the exception of an uncle that was autistic. I knew that the research around autism being inherited was unclear, and that a family history of autism didn't mean that my child would be born on the spectrum. Having a sperm donor, instead of a known donor, seemed to make more sense to me. Page wouldn't have to fear that the biological father would try to assert his rights. It was just a much easier process. The clinic suggested that we could do the insemination at the office, but we thought it would be more intimate to do it at home. They could mail the kit to us when I was ovulating, and we could do it ourselves, right in our bedroom. The statistics of at-home inseminations weren't very good—only about a 15 to 20 percent chance of getting pregnant—but I was familiar with the rates and knew that if I tracked my cycle properly, stayed healthy and stress-free, that my odds would dramatically increase. After all, the odds of a heterosexual couple getting pregnant in any given month is also only 15–20 percent. I knew the odds but I was also confident I would get pregnant on the first try. I'm an overachiever.

During this time, Page's youngest brother, Stan, came to visit us. This was his first time coming to visit. We told him that we were trying to get pregnant.

"Page, make sure you don't stress Nina out. That's important."

"Why is everyone telling me not to stress her out? I know."

I felt reassured that Page would be on her best behavior while I was pregnant. I had already seen a drastic change in her mood. Less mood swings. A more positive disposition.

Right before our first try at pregnancy, Page suggested we move. She wanted to feel like the place she lived was her house too. We were still living in my house, where Page was paying half the mortgage at this point. I understood what she meant. I would probably feel uncomfortable if I lived in a house that she owned. So, our hunt for an apartment began. I was excited. I felt that the walls of my house were tainted—full of bad memories that I wanted to forget. If we left the house, maybe the memories would fade. Maybe they would stay trapped in the house we left behind. It felt like an opportunity for a fresh start.

We decided to look for places in downtown Dallas, while I put my three-bedroom house up for rent. We needed an apartment that was okay with our cat, Charlie, living there, big enough for us and our new baby, with an outside space for Page to smoke her weed—the habit I lived with, but despised. I felt an outside space was important, because I knew Page would not be able to stop smoking weed and I didn't want to argue about it. I was absolutely against any weed smoke around my child or my pregnancy. The move would put both Page and I closer to our jobs, with the added benefit of a brand-new start in a new home. I'd also be getting an extra five hundred dollars a month in rental income from the house I owned. It was hard to find a place that met all our needs, but after looking at more than ten places, we found Cypress Creek Apartments.

A month after moving in, I was ovulating and ready to try the first round of sperm injections. The package came right on time. I would be inseminated by Page twice over a forty-eight-hour period. Once Page injected the sperm with the supplied syringe, we'd make love and I'd put my legs up for five minutes, to make sure the sperm traveled down the cervix. So that's what we did. The thought of bringing a child into the world even disarmed my previous disgust around having sex with Page. It felt like a new beginning. We were embarking on a new journey together. I believed Page would change, because she wanted a baby so badly. *Of course* she would change.

I didn't tell my mom about our plans to have a baby. I didn't want her to discourage me. I had made up my mind and I didn't need any naysayers. The stress could reduce my chances of getting pregnant and it wouldn't be good for my relationship with Page. Three weeks had passed since the insemination. I was at my house, soon to be a rental property, painting the main bedroom. It felt good to be in a place I owned and that I would now be making money from. I got good rental income—$1,600 a month. In college, I had rented lots of places from homeowners and it was always my dream to be on the other end, having a college student paying my mortgage. My tenants were moving in soon. A nice family—a couple with three kids. The father was a firefighter. The mother was an accountant. Page was at work but we had been arguing that day, so I wasn't speaking to her. The night before, we had been out at a party, having a good time. Suddenly and randomly, she'd told me that she was getting rid of the cable. At this point we split rent and she paid for the cable bill. I told her that it wasn't fair for her to arbitrarily make a decision for the entire household, without talking it over with me first. I didn't even understand how someone could think that was okay. But that was Page. It was also a glimpse into the monster that would be unleashed, with now living somewhere that she felt she had more of a say over. She didn't like that I was pushing back on the idea, and in the middle of the party, surrounded by all of her friends, she looked at me and said,

"Fuck you."

I wasn't sure if anyone else heard it. I had looked around in embarrassment, hoping no one had, and didn't see anyone looking in our direction. Page was now publicly humiliating me, something she hadn't done in the past. I immediately turned around and left the party. I took a cab home and she stayed out for another few hours. When she got home, I had no idea what time, I was asleep. The next morning, I showered, got dressed, and went back up to my rental property to finish painting. I didn't say a word to her.

By this point in our relationship, Page had decided to work from home. I'm not even sure that her employer allowed it, but she told me that everyone else on the job was working from home. I didn't probe; I'd learned to keep the peace whenever possible. She was still paying her share of the rent and some bills. As my thoughts drifted in and out, I decided to give Page a call. I missed her and wanted to tell her how the rental property clean-up was going. She always had great ideas about interior design and how to make the place look better—one of the things I loved about her. I valued her advice, since I wasn't the design type. I couldn't care less what color the walls were or how to match the countertops with the kitchen floor panels. Page loved that kind of stuff.

"Hey Page, how's work?"

"Good. Busy." She was brief.

"I miss you, but I really didn't like the way you talked to me about the cable thing. I know you've lived with people before. Why do you think it's okay to make a decision for the entire house on your own?" I was genuinely curious.

"Nina, what I said to you wasn't that bad. I even asked my friends if what I did was wrong. They said it wasn't that bad."

There are actually people who think that's okay? Maybe I am too sensitive.

"Lately, you've been doing the same thing your mom does to you," Page said.

"Huh? What's that?"

144

"She always jumps on you for small things and you're just like her. You don't like when she gets mad at you for not answering the phone, right? It's a small thing. Well, it's the same thing. You should think about that."

It happened so quickly. Out of nowhere, I felt a rage come over me. "I fucking hate you. You are a despicable person. I'd never want to have a child with someone who thinks it's okay to talk to me that way." I was screaming through the phone. I felt like all of my emotions over the last two years had bubbled up and exploded. I felt an anger that I had never felt before—it was actually scary. Had Page been in my presence at that moment, I didn't know what I would have done to her. I was exhibiting extreme emotions. I knew by now that Page thrived off of the roller coaster of volatility. In this moment, I realized two things: 1. My hormones were out of control and I might be pregnant. And 2. I most definitely had to leave Page.

If I am not pregnant, I'm gonna leave her. I am going to do it this time. For good. I was serious, but first I had to get a pregnancy test. I went to the nearest drugstore.

I took the test. It would leave a red strip if I was pregnant. After peeing on the stick in the restroom of the store and waiting thirty seconds, the stick was a faint pink.

Guess I'm not pregnant. It's not red. I was actually surprised. I always exceeded expectations. *How did I not get pregnant on the first try?* I took a picture of the results and sent them to my friend Steph.

"Hey Steph, what does this light pink strip mean?" I knew she would have some insight because she had four kids of her own.

"It means you're pregnant."

"Really? But it's so faint."

"Yeah, but any color is a positive."

I trusted her opinion. She was my go-to. The next time Steph would hear from me, the news wouldn't be so happy. I immediately called Page, but she didn't answer. I was so happy and excited to share my news that I texted three of my close friends and two of our mutual friends. They were so happy for us. When I got home later that day, Page was in the living room with a can of beer. She was now having beer delivered to the house. I saw a delivery man at the door as I was driving up the block toward the house.

"So, you told everyone but me that you were pregnant?"

"Well, I called you first but you didn't answer and I was excited."

"I got like five congratulations text messages from friends and I didn't even know you were pregnant."

I just walked past her to the bedroom and lay on the bed, staring at the ceiling. The moment I found out that I was pregnant should have been a happy memory. *Maybe it will get better*, I thought. *Page always says that we will get better with time. That's what happens in relationships—the more you know and learn someone, the better it gets.* Still, the rage I'd felt earlier that day had rattled me. I turned my head to the side and saw a vision board that I'd been working on. The scissors I had used to cut pictures out of old magazines lay on top of the poster board. *I should just stab her in the neck,* I thought. *That would rid me of this madness. No, I can't do that, then my future would be destroyed. I have to leave her,* I thought. *Why can't I just leave her?* The simultaneous yet contradictory thoughts put me in a space I had never consciously been before. I knew it wasn't just the hormones making me feel this way. I was reaching my breaking point and I had to do something about it, now.

Three months had gone by since the day I contemplated stabbing Page to death with a pair of scissors. It still haunted me. *I hope these thoughts don't transfer to my baby. I have to get my head in a better place*. I was just finishing up my first trimester and beginning to show. By now, my close family and friends knew I was pregnant. My mother was confused as to how a woman could have a baby without sleeping with a man. I simply told her to "Google it" when she asked me how sperm injected into my vagina could produce a baby. Ever since the cable incident, Page seemed to be transformed. She was cleaning Charlie's litter box for me, since I couldn't do it anymore; pregnant women shouldn't clean up cat litter, apparently. We hadn't argued at all. She would rub my feet when I asked. We would take long walks and talk about everything. It felt like we had just met. Sometimes, the butterflies would even come back.

The only thing that still caused tension was her smoking weed in the house. She had promised that she wouldn't while I was pregnant or after the baby was born. We also had an outdoor space for her to smoke her weed, so I wouldn't have to deal with it. But that didn't matter. One morning I had woken to Page sitting at the front door, blowing smoke outside, but the entire living room reeked of the smell. I was livid. I couldn't believe that she would smoke weed in the vicinity of a pregnant woman and not care.

By now, we had already agreed that we would go through the adoption process, but I was having second thoughts about it. I told her that I wouldn't be completing the adoption process until I was confident that she could get her act together. She was still having alcohol delivered to the house every other day and didn't care enough about me or the baby to give us a smoke-free house. Page, surprisingly, didn't push back too much on this idea. But she did tell me that she knew she had no rights as the child's legal parent if we didn't go through with what is called a second-parent adoption. In Texas, if you are married and have a child as a lesbian couple, you qualify to allow your partner, the non-biological spouse, to adopt the baby. I was already seven months pregnant. The baby and I were doing great. I had stayed up all hours of the night throughout my pregnancy making sure that adoption was the only surefire way Page could be the legal parent of my child. I must have read literally hundreds of legal blogs and articles. I knew if Page didn't change her ways, I would have to get my baby away from her. I was willing to give her a chance, but I also knew at this point that I needed to do what was best for myself and my unborn child. Something in me had shifted. I wasn't hanging the adoption over her head because I was trying to use it as leverage for her to change—I was doing it for my baby. Without an adoption, if I decided to leave her after the baby was born, she'd have no legal recourse or rights to my child. At least, that's what I thought.

"Babies will change you," Steph said one night on the phone.

"Yeah, I know," I said.

But I didn't know. I didn't have a baby yet. What I felt then didn't compare to what I felt when baby Chasten was born. He was

already changing me, but that was just the
beginning.

YEAR 4: 2021

"It is easier to build strong children than to repair broken men."
-- Frederick Douglass

During my third trimester, I agreed to take the next step in the adoption process, which was to get married. Page had started going to therapy and seemed to be trying. This was a major sign to me that she was serious about changing her ways, but I remained skeptical. I never wanted to get married, but I did want to be fair to Page. I felt I needed to do everything I could to make sure Page felt like a parent, because if she felt insecure about her role as a parent, it would backfire and lead to more problems. I told Page that I didn't want an actual wedding. I just wanted to go down to the Justice of the

Peace with a few people present. For me, this wasn't a celebration. It was a means to an end.

The night before the ceremony, I was very emotional. At about midnight, I began to cry in bed. I thought it was just hormones and that it would quickly pass. But it didn't. I started to cry uncontrollably. Page tried to comfort me but I pushed her away. I had never cried like this in my entire life. The only other time I remember even coming close was when I learned that my grandmother who suffered from dementia didn't remember my name. As I cried, I wanted to call so many people. To tell them that it wasn't that I didn't want to get married, but that I didn't want to get married to Page. That I was making the worst mistake of my life. The way I cried was divine. I'd learn later that any time an uncontrollable emotion comes over you, especially if it is a once in a lifetime feeling, that it actually is the universe guiding you away from a really bad mistake. A mistake that will not just change your life, but the lives of others. A mistake that will alter the trajectory of your path. But my world was so small at this point. I hadn't confided in anyone. I felt I had no one to call who would understand. I looked at my phone to call Mel, but I hadn't talked to him in more than four months. Page was the only one who kept up with him consistently. *He wouldn't want to hear from me*, I thought.

"I don't want to do it. You're so mean," I sobbed. I must have repeated the words "you're so mean" a million times— somewhere deep down inside, hoping she would grasp how badly she had treated me over the years. I was a wreck. Page told me that she would leave the house, so I could think about my decision. She was calm. Emotionless. In retrospect, she was calculating the situation. Gauging how she could convince me to go through with it. She knew leaving would give me a sense of loneliness. I was extremely vulnerable. She knew me well enough to know that I would just beg her to stay. That's the sickness of abuse for the victim. The abused sympathizes with the abuser. Still, at this time, abuse wasn't the way that I characterized the relationship. She reminded me that she was there for me and just wanted the best for our family. As she went to open the front door of the house, I cried hysterically for her to stay. She stopped, looked over at me, and approached the couch that I was sitting on. She sat gently next to me and held me as I sobbed. It's unexplainable, to want only the person who is hurting you to be the one to console you.

"I want you to stay, but I just want to go to bed. I'll be fine in the morning."

So, when I was eight months pregnant, we went to downtown Dallas and got married in front of my mom, dad, and brothers. On our wedding day, it was a frigid day by Dallas standards, fifty degrees and cloudy. I was bundled up tightly as I walked into the courthouse with my mom by my side. Page was spending the morning with her father and aunt who had come down for the Justice of the Peace ceremony. We had agreed to meet at the courthouse one hour before the ceremony. It was thirty minutes past the hour and Page hadn't arrived yet.

I knew she would show up, and it didn't surprise me that she was running behind. I had accepted that punctuality wasn't one of Page's strong points. A couple of minutes before we were called in, Page crept up behind me as I waited in the hall, pacing back and forth.

"Hey baby, ready for the big day?" she said with a large grin on her face.

I nervously smiled. Her breath smelled like alcohol.

We stood before the officiant, who seemed to be genuinely happy for us. Same-sex marriage had just been legalized across the country within the last five years, so I took the officiant's excitement to be his support of same-sex unions in general. We stood before the judge.

"Friends, we have been invited here today to share with Nina Chandler and Page Bell a very important moment in their lives..." I was shaking as the officiant read his script. I couldn't even look Page in the eyes, but I knew I had to find the strength to go through with it. I couldn't call the wedding off in the middle of the ceremony. I contemplated in my head the options I had to wiggle out of this. If I backed out now, I'd look like a fool. I'd be embarrassed and I would embarrass Page. I was in too deep; I had to go through with it. Besides, I wasn't a quitter. The next thing I remember is the officiant saying,

"Ms. Chandler, do you take Page Bell as your lawfully wedded wife, to have and to hold,   from this day forward..."

My voice was hesitant and shaky. I glanced at my mom, who was looking on, but made sure not to really look her in the eyes, since I didn't want to break down crying. I shed a tear and left my fate up to hope. To an outsider, I was crying out of happiness. Inside, I was crying out of fear. I was caught in a cycle of willingly giving my power away, for reasons I couldn't explain then and can't explain today.

"I do."

Page, wiggling her legs back and forth like an excited toddler, smiled and said "I do."

"You may kiss the bride."

We were married.

I didn't invite any of my friends to the ceremony, nor did I tell them about it. Even though I knew this might be hurtful, they'd understand one day, I reasoned. I only invited my parents and brothers because I knew I had to. If I got married without telling my mom, she would lose it. Page was so happy during the celebration dinner afterward. She seemed relaxed. My mom was quiet the entire dinner. Page's father stood up and spoke. He said he considered me to already be a part of the family and that he loved me. His remarks weren't surprising. I liked Page's father; I thought he was a sweet old man and he treated me like a daughter. For now, at least.

The last few weeks of pregnancy, the smell of Page's skin made me nauseous. Her pores constantly smelled like processed alcohol and her neck seemed to always be sweaty. She also complained about pins and needles in her hands. A complaint I had heard her make before. I had stayed up many nights over the last few months, researching the effects of alcohol on the body. I was convinced at this point that Page didn't just have an alcohol problem, but that she was an alcoholic. At this point, it seemed as if there were always empty beer bottles piled up in the kitchen trash and in the recycle bin, but I never asked her about it. I just hoped once the baby got here, she'd stop, like she'd promised. She even told me that she was just getting her last licks in before the baby came because she was "fully committed to an alcohol-free and drug-free life once the baby is here."

This reassured me. Hope is a powerful thing. It can keep you in a dire situation; it can also get you out of a dire situation. For me, it was the former. I tried to convince myself that therapy would fix her.

At eight and a half months pregnant, my worst nightmare came to pass. It was two a.m. and another unusually cold Friday night when my phone rang. Since I was due within the next couple of weeks, my job had given me twelve weeks off, in addition to the two weeks prior to my due date So, thankfully, I had at least: six weeks for recovery and six weeks for baby bonding time. It was the morning of my second day of leave.

"Hello...Page?

"What's my address? I need to get home, what's my address, Nina?" She was completely trashed.

"Put the cab driver on the phone."

A part of me was so concerned that she wouldn't make it home safely, and another part of me wanted her to get in a terrible car accident on the way home and die. I felt horrible for my thoughts, yet at this point, I was so deluded that hoping she'd die seemed more reasonable than just leaving her. I had dug myself deeper into this dysfunctional relationship.

"1512 Claymont Avenue. I'll be outside waiting."

"Okay, thank you," the cab driver said.

I got up, threw a heavy jacket on, and walked to the corner so that I could see the cab when it came toward the block. We lived on a small side street that was hard to find through all the bends, turns, and hills of the area. It was an apartment complex, but it looked like a community of fancy row homes. Our street was like a picturesque alley. GPS never brought people directly to the door, only to the corner. Our house sat in the middle of an incline, on a hill. I was so scared. My stomach sat so far out, it looked like I could deliver the baby at any time. After about ten minutes, the cab driver pulled up to the corner where I was standing. He got out and came around to Page's door. He opened it for her and she literally fell out of the car onto the sidewalk. I recognized that this was an extremely dangerous situation for me. It was fifty degrees and the rain made the ground so slippery. I wished the cab driver would offer assistance, but he didn't. He barely made eye contact with me, before turning to run back to the driver's seat and pulling away. He wanted no part of this situation.

"Get up, Page. I can't pick you up. I'm too pregnant and if I fall, I will have to go to the ER. You are going to have to walk on your own," I said sternly.

She slowly stood, her knees buckling as I looked on. As she took a step toward our block, she quickly bent over to throw up.

"Turn your head. I don't want you to see me like this."

She even cares how this is affecting me, while completely intoxicated and barely conscious, I thought. *This must mean she truly cares about me, deep, deep down inside.* I suffered from affirmation bias, when it came to Page—using anything to affirm that she actually did love me. We eventually made it to the house. She stumbled up the stairs to the bed. She passed out, while I sat outside the bedroom doorway on the floor, looking at her. I didn't know what to do. I was exhausted but couldn't get into bed next to her. She was sprawled out across the entire bed and would sleep way too wildly for me to sleep with her. I just looked at her, contemplating. She popped her head up.

"Baby? You there?"

I didn't respond. She then vomited red-pinkish liquid all over the bed. I started to cry. The house only had two bedrooms. The other bedroom was set up for the baby. There was nowhere else for me to sleep but a tiny sofa in the living room. I was too big and too pregnant to sleep there.

"Page, get up! You threw up all over the bed," I yelled.

She sat on the side of the bed and slowly stood up. I continued to cry in disbelief. She went into the bathroom and turned on the bathtub faucet. She was running herself a bath. As the water ran, she looked down at the tub and lost her footing, grabbing onto the shower curtain as she fell into the tub. Now, she was naked, in the tub, with the water running and the broken shower curtain and rod in the water with her. I walked in to turn the water off, as she lay sleeping in the tub. *It's not my job to fix this*, I thought. I grabbed my phone and took pictures of her in the tub, as well as the vomit-covered bed. I'd show her the pictures when she was sober. Maybe then she would finally see and really understand what I had to deal with.

"I'm leaving for the night. I don't have anywhere to sleep and I'm so tired." I quickly turned on my computer and found the best penthouse suite in the city. If I was going to sleep out of the house as a pregnant woman, after what I'd had to deal with, I was going to at least have a night in luxury. I booked my room, made it to the penthouse, and went to sleep.

The next morning when I woke up, I texted my cousin Baraki. I told him what had happened and where I was. I sent him the pictures I had taken of Page. I revealed to him that this has been ongoing and that Page really had a problem. Surprisingly, it felt liberating to finally give someone a glimpse into what I was dealing with privately. At least I'm in a penthouse, only the best, I joked with Marc over text message. After seeing the pictures, he immediately called me.

"She really needs to get it together."

"What are you gonna do?"

He lived in NYC, so it wasn't as if he could offer any immediate help.

"I don't know."

It was a brief conversation. Around one p.m., my phone rang—Page.

"Where are you?"

"I'm at a hotel. Last night you threw up all over the bed. I won't be back until you fix the shower curtain, wash the sheets, and clean up the bed. Call me back when you finish."

"Okay."

I could tell by her tone that she remembered nothing of the night. I walked around the hotel, checking out the pool, sitting in the park on the rooftop, reading magazines. Just trying to relax and figure out what I needed to do or say to Page. By four p.m., I was already missing her. Wishing she was at the hotel with me. You might ask why. That's a good question, and I can't answer it to anyone's satisfaction—not even mine. One of the things I have come to understand about abuse is that my response is not atypical. But it would take an expert in psychology to explain how these things can happen and why victims respond the way they do. I texted Page the address to the hotel and told her to come by.

"You gotta see this place." I wanted her to see how cool the hotel was. Page made her way to the hotel around six p.m. She walked through the room door with a somber disposition. I gave her a hug and kiss on the cheek. I don't know if it was the pregnancy hormones, the comfortability with the cycle of dysfunction, or both, but I missed her. I just wanted her to get better. If she could do that then everything could work out. Hope.

"You really need to get help. Last night was so scary. Do you even remember anything?"

174

"I remember getting in the cab. I remember waking up this morning in the bathtub. That's it, really."

I pulled out my phone to show her the pictures I had taken of her.

"This is what happened."

"You took pictures of me? Why would you do that? Why would you take pictures of anyone in a vulnerable state like that? It's just wrong."

"I wanted you to see what I had to deal with. So that you can get help. I thought maybe these would show you that you need help."

I felt bad for taking the pictures when I saw her reaction, but I felt it was the only way for her to see that she truly had a drinking

175

problem. My guilt stemming from years of putting her feelings before my own. I gave her an ultimatum. If she didn't go into an alcohol treatment program, then I would not go through with the adoption ever. Page agreed to start a program before the baby came. That meant that she had only a couple of weeks to start her sessions. In the meantime, I put the adoption paperwork on hold indefinitely.

On February 21, 2021, baby Chasten Chandler Bell was born at 12:06 a.m. I didn't mind giving baby Chasten her last name, because my connection with Chasten could never be denied, and I wanted to make sure she would feel just as connected to the baby as I did. I knew she was insecure about not only her role in the process of having a baby, but also other deep, dark things that I would never know. Also, I assumed that I could always change his last name, if we broke up. I thought this would help her bond with the baby and put a fire under her butt to get healthy. I also thought that her desire to officially adopt Chasten would surely help her get her act together. My heart superseded any objective thought, as is sometimes the case with love. During the delivery, my mom and Page were in the room. I gave birth to baby Chasten naturally, in a tub of water. I was scared. I didn't know what to expect. I always knew it would be painful, but I didn't know how painful until I actually went through it. Chasten came after about four hours of labor and two hours of pushing. It was arduous. I probably should have gotten a C-section and an epidural but I was determined to push him out naturally, in the tub. The only way I can describe labor is a feeling of being half alive and half dead at the same time. When it comes to labor, it can go either way—you might die pushing or you might live pushing. At least that's what it felt like for me. During the labor, for a moment, my mother and Page got along, but that wouldn't last long. A few days before I went into labor, I had asked my aunt what it felt like. She told me that it wasn't that bad and that it just felt like a really big poop. Obviously, every woman's experience is different. After giving it all I had, through the blood, sweat, and tears, baby Chasten was ready to be brought into the world and I was ready to give him the world. Having a baby is truly a team effort on the part of mother and child. The baby has to try its best to come out and you have to try your best to push him out, in tandem, together. One doesn't work without the other.

I'd carried Chasten for nine months. I'd gotten to know him and he had gotten to know me, from the inside out. When he was delivered, Page cut the umbilical cord and my mother shouted out the gender. We had planned that Page would shout out the gender, so when my mom screamed "It's a boy!" before her, Page cut her eyes at my mom as if she wanted to kill her. I was numb to everything. I was so exhausted and disappointed. It was a sobering reality that nothing could change the dysfunctional dynamic within my family. But Baby Chasten was here now. He was real. It was my job to protect him. My job to raise him and my job to nourish him. I would give my life to protect his. I decided to strictly breastfeed him for the first nine months. Breastfeeding is not for the faint of heart. It's hard, but I was persistent.

Three weeks had passed since baby Chasten was born. Page was acting sporadic and angry. Uncooperative and erratic. Since his birth, she had been even more of a nightmare than at any other time in our relationship. The first week after coming home from the hospital is a big blur in my memory, with the exception of the pain. I probably blocked out how awful life in the house with Page really was. I channeled all of my energy and focus onto Chasten. I do, however, remember the pain. My legs and ankles were swollen due to postpartum edema, where the excess fluid from pregnancy has to slowly drain out of the body. My vagina hurt too. A six-pound, twelve-ounce human was pushed from between my legs. My mom would come over often to rub my feet and make meals. Page didn't even try to hide her disdain for my mother anymore. Looking back, I know it infuriated her that she couldn't completely isolate me from my mom.

Mostly, I remember staring at baby Chasten in amazement for the first few weeks. Nothing else mattered, except him. The pain, the sleeplessness, and the exhaustion were all worth it, for him. I grappled with the type of people I wanted him to be around and the type of life I wanted to give him. Page was not someone I wanted my son to be around. This became more and more clear as the days went on. It was real now. Everything mattered.

During this time, I was reminded how much support and love I had. My aunt, friends, brothers, cousins and distant relatives came frequently in those early days of Chasten's life. I was becoming stronger. Things were becoming clearer. I was seeing life through the eyes of my son. Page seemed to be completely in love with Chasten, yet hostile toward me. She was attentive toward him. She smiled, laughed, and played with him.

One night, after putting Chasten in a small baby tub on the counter to bathe him, he cried. He hated the water. The doctors had warned us that babies typically hated bathing at this age. So, I wasn't alarmed. I would make it quick. Suddenly, Page came storming into the bathroom.

"You're burning him!" She reached her hand into the water. "The water's too hot. You're burning him." She snatched the baby from my grip and removed him from the water.

I looked at her in disgust. I didn't respond, but I could see right through her. I'll never know for sure, but even today I believe she was trying to paint me as a negligent mother, in order to alienate me from my baby—or worse, paint me as unstable, with the intent of taking Chasten from me. The blinders were coming off. Even though he was an infant, my son had already taught me to trust my intuition. Trust my gut.

The second week home with Chasten, Page spent a lot of time outside smoking. It bothered me and I'd finally realized that it didn't matter how much I wanted her to change. She was who she was. There was no room to put her first anymore; Chasten occupied that spot now. Nothing was more important than him. They say babies change you, and my baby sure did change me. There was nothing that Page could say to me to make me lose my cool. I had no emotion toward her. A person can endure much suffering, if they believe it is for a purpose. I no longer saw the purpose that Page served in my life – in our lives. When Chasten was three weeks old, I woke him up to breastfeed him. When sleeping babies won't wake up to feed, you have to give them a little nudge. I sat outside on our patio, enjoying the weather with him and Page. It was time for him to eat and I was trying to wake him. Chasten, woozy and tired, half-opened his eyes, then

184

fell right back into a deep sleep. I looked at him in awe. I hadn't taken my eyes off of him since he'd been born. I had never felt anything like it. I understood love in an entirely different way now.

"Baby Chasten, baby, wake up. Mommy's gonna take your clothes off if you don't wake up to eat." My thoughts of bliss were abruptly broken.

"You're threatening him! Stop threatening him!"

My mouth dropped open. "What are you talking about?! And lower your voice! Why would you say I am threatening my baby? Are you crazy, Page?" I felt a surge of anger toward her; however, I didn't react. I went quiet, remembering that any type of reaction would affect the baby. I didn't want him to grow up with a warped sense of how you talk to others, especially loved ones. He was a mixed-race baby boy and the way he dealt with stress and anger mattered. Society would already see him as a threat because of his complexion. Boys of color had to learn early how to remain cool and non-threatening.

"You aren't fit to be a parent and you aren't fit to be my wife," I said in a completely calm and tranquil voice, now breastfeeding Chasten. "You accuse me of threatening my child because I joke about taking his clothes off?"

Page retorted, "You must have Asperger's."

She'd told me that I was autistic in the past.

186

"You have a mental condition," she said while I held Chasten.

I didn't respond to her. Her words bounced off of me like bullets hitting a bulletproof vest. There was nothing she could say to me, to get the reaction she wanted. Those days were over. *I've got to get us out of here.* It was harder to leave now that I had a baby. The thought was scary. Knowing you have to leave. Acknowledging that the situation you are in, is one that you created for yourself. Then blaming yourself and feeling bad for blaming yourself. It's not to say you are to blame, but instead to say that you can endure great pain, if you believe that it is purposeful. Envisioning peeling back all the layers of dysfunction that you have cloaked yourself in for the last few years. The thoughts, the thoughts, the thoughts cycled rapidly through my head like the ball in a pin ball machine. But this was no game.

After nursing him, I went back in the house. Page trailed behind me quietly. I took Chasten up to his crib, turned on the baby monitor, and closed his door. After eating, he would sleep for at least two hours, until it was time for the next feeding. That was when I got my breaks. It also happened to be my birthday. March 26, 2021. A day that I will never forget. I hadn't planned anything for my birthday because I was too wrapped up in being a mom.

Page said she was going downtown for her first intake at the treatment center, which included a screening and a game plan for treatment. She hadn't started before the baby came, like she'd said she would, and I had no confidence that she would actually follow through. I didn't want to waste my time going with her. If she wanted to get better, she had to do it herself. I was physically still living with her, but mentally I was completely gone. Whether or not she got treatment for her alcohol problem or not, I knew what I had to do. My entire life force was now focused on baby Chasten and what was best for him. Her appointment was at five p.m. and she was only supposed to be a few hours. I had a few family members and friends visit to bring me gifts and say happy birthday. My dad brought over a small chocolate birthday cake and a card. After the visits stopped and I was alone with Chasten, I realized that it was already ten p.m. *Where's Page? I know she didn't go out and get drunk.*

That would be crazy. As soon as I entertained the thought, Page came barreling through the door. For some reason, I can still vividly hear the sound of the front door violently crashing into the wall as she pushed her way into the house that night. She stumbled upstairs, right past baby Chasten and I. The stench turned my stomach into a knot. I sat, stunned, on the sofa with the baby as he dozed in and out of sleep. That was it. I called Page's father.

"I'm leaving Page and I'm not coming back. She's going to be upset and I'm scared. I'm calling you because maybe you can help her through this."

"Okay," her father said.

That phone call would be the last time I ever spoke to him.

I ran to the closet and retrieved a backpack for me and one for the baby. I collected my work laptop, cell phone, and wallet. I threw a few onesies in the bag for Chasten and some diapers, wipes. Truthfully, I didn't want to leave the house without telling her that I was leaving, because I didn't want her to wake up with no one in the house. If I did that, I knew she would just tell me what an awful person I was. That's the mindset of someone who has been manipulated and abused for years. The old me would have gone to wake her up to talk about it, but this, this was the new me.

After kissing Chasten on the forehead, I whispered in his tiny ear, "Mommy's gonna get us out of here my love. You deserve better."

I went upstairs to get my breast pump and saw Page lying on the bed with only a bathrobe on. I ran downstairs quietly, with baby Chasten in tow and the two backpacks. I heard Page's phone ringing but didn't think anything of it. I later found out that the ringing phone I heard was Page's father calling to tell her that I was leaving—which prompted her to storm after me in a rage.

That night was the beginning of the end. It ended with Page in handcuffs in the back of a police car and baby Chasten and I finally going to the only place that was safe— my mother's house. Once I left, I didn't look back. Three weeks later, I filed for divorce. We had only been married for seven months. This is not to say that leaving for good was easy. Sometimes when I least expect it, I see the tip of a kitchen knife over my head or I hear the slamming of the front door as if I am actually living in my past. Living the experiences over and over again. Sometimes I cry. Not because of what happened to me but because of what I let happen to myself. Because I didn't think enough of myself to say to Page, "fuck you" and mean it. Because the most beautiful thing was born out of the most heinous four years of my entire life but sometimes it's like that, I guess. Isnt that what they mean when they say, when life gives you lemons, make lemonade?

A few days after leaving, I picked up a copy of the police report I had filed. I read through the report and noticed that at the end it said "victim should report to 342 Maple Avenue, to get a PFA." I plugged the address into the Google search bar—it was the location of the Sumneytown Domestic Abuse Unit. My eyebrows scrunched together. It hadn't hit me yet. *Domestic Abuse Unit*, I whispered. I then searched the letters "PFA" and learned that PFA stood for Protection Against Abuse order.

"Let me read the report," I heard a voice say.

I handed it to my mom, and she read through it. I don't even think she noticed the almost illegible scribblings at the end of the report.

"It says I should go get an order of protection for us."

"Has Page ever done anything like this before Nina?"

I looked over at Chasten, who was sleeping in his motorized swing with not a care in the world.

"Mom, she was an a-a-a—an abuser." I had finally said the words out loud to someone else. It was the first time. Page was an abuser. I told my mom the details of the night I left her. I told her how Page had chased us outside and tried to take Chasten out of the car. I told her how frightened I was. I told her that Page had pulled a knife on me. I told her everything. My mom, typically quite stoic and emotionless, a result of being a strong Black woman I suppose, looked at me intently, with a mix of rage, sadness, and guilt. I stared back at her, as vulnerable as a toddler. I needed her now more than ever. It's a funny thing, vulnerability. It can bring so much clarity when expressed to someone who actually loves you in the way you should be loved. Life, however, doesn't dictate when or who you should be vulnerable with. It is up to you to make that decision for yourself. In that sense, it's true – wisdom comes with experience. I was still, at that point, struggling to see myself as a victim of abuse though - another label. Labels come with identities and identities come with stigmas and stigmas have consequences. So, that was hard for me. As much as I thought I had my life together, I had to come to terms with the fact that I had allowed myself to be in an emotionally, verbally, and physically abusive relationship. One that I could have left long ago. But before I went through it, I didn't even know female-on-female domestic abuse was a thing. Would having known that changed anything anyway? All I knew now was that Chasten needed me. I knew that for sure.

"Pack the baby up, I'll drive you down there."

Me, my mom, and Chasten headed to the Domestic Abuse Unit to get a PFA. As I sat in the passenger seat of my mom's car, I stared out of the window, my mind full of questions, but not many answers. I was fearful about what the future held for me and my baby. *Were we truly safe now? Would the Domestic Abuse Unit believe me? Was it enough for a PFA?* I looked down at my phone. I had thirteen missed calls from Page and five missed calls from an unknown number. When I saw her name scroll across my cell phone screen, I had only one thought: Chasten deserves better.

As I thought about the future, I wondered how I would explain Chasten's early years to him. I wondered if Page would try to take Chasten from me. I was scared and uncertain, but grateful and resolved. Had it not been for baby Chasten, I never would have left her—a fact that I'd spend the next several years trying to unpack. A fact that I had to seriously reckon with. As I look back on my relationship with Page, I realize that Chasten gave me strength. Love is strength. My mother taught me how to love and my child taught me how to be loved. As Chasten grows, I'll be honest with him about how he was brought into this world. I'll teach him to value himself, to love himself and that he matters. That his feelings matter. That we matter. I'll teach him how to grow into a man that others are blessed to live among.

THE END.

A note from the author:

Say Something, Do Something

If you think you are in an abusive relationship, you probably are. There are resources available. Abuse can take many forms, and many forms of abuse can go ignored. Abusers want to control and have power over their victims. Too often, the abused, after years of abuse, lash out at their abuser, and as a result they are considered a participant in the abusive behavior. Trying to regain your humanity and control over your own life is not abuse. Reactive abuse does not exist.

If you or someone you know, needs help, please call your local abuse hotline or, in the United States, call the National Domestic Abuse hotline number at **1-800-799-SAFE**

(7233). Finally, if you notice any signs of emotional, verbal or physical abuse towards one of your loved ones: Say something, Do something. Your loved one may be suffering in silence.

Other books by Sheena C. Howard:

Black Comics: Politics of Race and Representation (Bloomsbury Press)

Black Queer Identity Matrix (Peter Lang Press)

Encyclopedia of Black Comics (Fulcrum Publishing)

Critical Articulation of Race, Gender and Sexual Orientation (Lexington Press)

Superb: A Comic Book (Lion Forge)

If you want to support me – the author, please do the following:

- Find *Nina's Whisper* on Amazon, Kindle and Audible and **leave a review.**

- Buy a copy of *Nina's Whisper* for a friend.

- Buy an extra copy of *Nina's Whisper* for yourself.

- Recommend *Nina's Whisper* to anyone and everyone.

- Find me on social media at: Dr. Sheena Howard.

- Blog about *Nina's Whisper*.

- Tweet about *Nina's Whisper*.

- Write a Facebook post about *Nina's Whisper*.

- Find me on Patreon.com and support me monthly – even 3 dollars a month helps.

- Tag me on social media, using #ninaswhisper or with an image of the book cover.

- Share your purchase of the book or image of the book on your social media.

About the Author

Sheena C. Howard is an award-winning author, filmmaker and scholar, including a 2014 Eisner Award for her co-edited book, *Black Comics: Politics of Race and Representation*. In 2016, she directed, produced and wrote the documentary *Remixing Colorblind*, and she has bylines *in The Huffington Post, Curve Magazine, Philadelphia Inquirer* and more. She is dedicated to telling stories that typically go untold. She believes that everyone can learn from the stories and experiences of others.